STEALING HOMER

To John + Joann
Best wishes

Stealing Homer

A Rascal Harbor Mystery

Geoffrey Scott

Prospective Press
Winston-Salem

PROSPECTIVE PRESS LLC
1959 Peace Haven Rd, #246, Winston-Salem, NC 27106 U.S.A.
www.prospectivepress.com

Published in the United States of America by PROSPECTIVE PRESS LLC

🛆 TRADEMARK

STEALING HOMER
A RASCAL HARBOR MYSTERY
Text copyright © S. G. Grant, 2018
All rights reserved.
The author's moral rights have been asserted.

Cover and interior design by ARTE RAVE
Copyright © Prospective Press LLC, 2018
All rights reserved.
The copyright holder's moral rights have been asserted.

ISBN 978-1-943419-70-8

First PROSPECTIVE PRESS trade paperback edition

Printed in the United States of America
First printing, April, 2018

1 3 5 7 9 10 8 6 4 2

The text of this book was typeset in Caslon Pro
Accent text was typeset in Belleza

PUBLISHER'S NOTE

This book is a work of fiction. The people, names, characters, locations, activities, and events portrayed or implied by this book are the product of the author's imagination or are used fictitiously. Any resemblance to actual people, locations, and events is strictly coincidental. No actual paintings were harmed in the writing of this novel.

Without limiting the rights as reserved in the above copyright, no part of this publication may be reproduced, stored in or introduced into any retrieval system, or transmitted—by any means, in any form, electronic, mechanical, photocopying, recording, or otherwise—without the prior written permission of the publisher. Not only is such reproduction illegal and punishable by law, but it also hurts the author who toiled hard on the creation of this work and the publisher who brought it to the world. In the spirit of fair play, and to honor the labor and creativity of the author, we ask that you purchase only authorized electronic and print editions of this work and refrain from participating in or encouraging piracy or electronic piracy of copyright-protected materials. Please give authors a break and don't steal this or any other work.

Cover contains an image © S. G. Grant. Used with permission.

Acknowledgments

Writing a novel means the author spends lots of private time. Conceiving, drafting, editing, re-editing, and the like is largely solitary work. At some point, however, the private work turns public as drafts are shared, read, and discussed. The private work is, by turns, exhilarating, exhausting, enervating, and enlightening. The public work is just scary, as it invariably feels like sudden and dramatic exposure.

Friendly readers help. For me, that list includes Emily Cole, Jean Dorak, Jenny Gordon, Ardeanna Hamlin, and Alison Insinna. In reading parts of or the whole manuscript, each offered kind words and thoughtful feedback…and more kind words. They might not have had the chance to even read the book, however, if the first airing in front of my family had not produced a consensus reaction: "Gee, that's not too bad!" Inspiration need not be deep to still be inspiring…

In addition to those named above, I single out for special thanks my editor and publisher Jason Graves. Not only did Jason take on the burden of a rookie novelist, but his clear, patient, and attentive guidance enriched *Stealing Homer* on every level. Thanks, Jason.

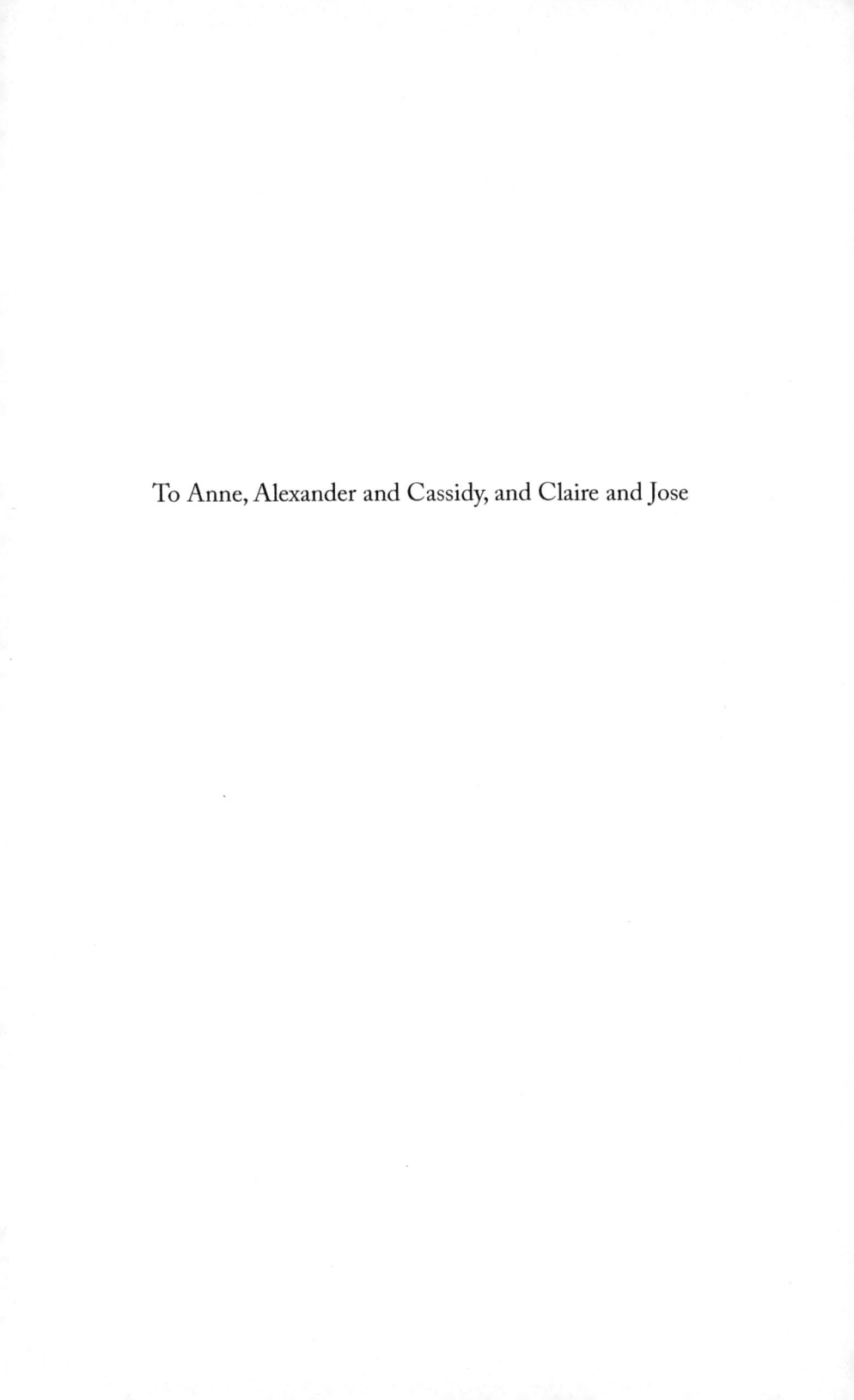

To Anne, Alexander and Cassidy, and Claire and Jose

CHAPTER 1

"Honest to Christ, that kid's got himself in a pickle now. Idiot." John McTavish soon learned that the idiot was Jimmy Park and the pickle was a stolen Winslow Homer painting. The concerned citizen was Gary Park, Jimmy's dad, and proprietor of the imaginatively named Gary's Garage.

McTavish happened to be Gary's audience on a brilliant, late fall morning when he learned of his son's predicament. Gary's strained and silent face cued McTavish in to the seriousness of the problem. His single interjection, "Jesus, Jimmy," underscored that conclusion. Jimmy Park had somehow managed to be arrested for stealing a newly discovered Winslow Homer watercolor.

Gary's quiet, on-phone countenance broke as soon as the connection did. Calling on Jesus and defining the problem as a "pickle" were just the beginning. Gary recounted the call with comments that were in equal part editorial, obscene, and thinly veiled love.

"Jesus, Jesus, Jesus. That boy has gotten himself in one blue fart of a situation," Gary said.

McTavish waited.

"Somehow, the idiot got arrested for stealing that paintin' they were showin' last night over at the gallery. The one by that guy...you know, the guy?"

"The one by Winslow Homer?" McTavish asked. "Jimmy stole the Homer?"

"Yup, yup, that's it." Gary nodded. "The one they found in that attic. And…holy Christ, I can't even believe I'm sayin' this…but they're sayin' Jimmy swiped it. The damn idiot. What the hell would he do that for?"

"No idea," McTavish said helplessly. Jimmy—or James as he now preferred to be called—and McTavish had spent long hours talking about art as they shared an affinity for watercolor in general and for Winslow Homer and Andrew Wyeth in particular. In each case, what McTavish liked was that their work held meaning below the surface-level clarity of the images.

The classic example is Andrew Wyeth's *Christina's World*. That now-iconic image, at a distance, evokes the dreamy past, present, and future of a young farm girl. Closer inspection of any piece of art almost always pays off. In Wyeth's painting, closer inspection upends the narrative. Christina's thin arms and awkward positioning might represent a young, still developing teen. The hands, however, belie the lie; these are the cramped and withered hands of the real Christina, a middle-aged woman with genetic polyneuropathy. There is no bait and switch here: Wyeth gives viewers all the facts. How they put them together—and then put them together again—is on them.

Such were the conversations in which Jimmy and McTavish engaged. Jimmy, the more talkative due to genetics and youthful passion; McTavish, the quieter due to a life-time disposition toward listening and a fear that he didn't have all that much interesting to say.

"Where is he?" McTavish asked. With no reasonable conjecture to explain Jimmy's alleged action, Gary moved on to the matter of helping his son.

"They got him in a cell down to Portland. Guess it was the Portland police that found the paintin' and picked him up. Jesus…maybe I just ought to let the boy stay there. Might smarten him up a little. Oh, but Ruby would have my ass. 'You got no very large clue about him,'" Gary said, aping Ruby's grating voice and tortured English. "I understand him all right. I just don't know how he could be *my* boy. You know?"

McTavish did, sort of, but there was a lot behind Gary's comment. Part of it was how Jimmy, an artist by nature and disposition, seemed so at odds with his father's practical minded, do-something-real approach toward life. Another part of it was Jimmy's determination to go to college, a path Gary had rejected for himself. And yet another part, a really big part, was Jimmy's seeming homosexuality. "Seeming" because, although Jimmy showed "signs" according to Gary, he had yet to come out. Jimmy and McTavish had talked around the issue any number of times. Jimmy "wondered" if McTavish knew any gay people. He talked about how much he hated his mother's fashion sense and about his father's angry reaction on overhearing Jimmy's suggestion that Ruby wear a bright purple scarf to "accent her dress and her eyes." And, during their art talks, Jimmy invariably brought up works created by known gay artists. As it turns out, McTavish did know a number of gay folks; he, too, thought Ruby's attire could use some help; and he admired the work of some gay artists, though he couldn't say it was because of whom they loved.

Jimmy's struggles were not lost on McTavish. For Jimmy to choose college over a job in his father's garage was hard. To choose an art major rather than something more practical was harder still. Layering on the struggle over his sexuality, well, that's a lot for any young man to face. Facing it with a loving, but largely clueless mother and a loving, but vaguely angry father left the boy Jimmy and the young adult James in McTavish's living room drinking too much coffee and talking late into the night. That this boy was now sitting in a jail cell for art theft seemed like one more, very big hill to climb.

His mixed feelings churning across his face, Gary nevertheless put the wheels in motion to get Jimmy out of jail. Julian Pratt, local lawyer and town snob, picked up Gary's call on the third ring. "Answering the phone yourself are you, squire?" Gary asked, his voice rough. "Where the hell is Martha?"

"Martha is on her extended lunch break, which leaves the task of talking with the town miscreants to me. Which of my many services do you need today, Mr. Park? Please *do* let me know how I can make your day better."

"Cut the shit, Julian," Gary said with emotion. "Jimmy's got himself in a goddamn mess." Several minutes and much swearing later, Gary had explained Jimmy's predicament and had asked Julian to represent him. Julian dawdled over the decision, but eventually agreed. Putting the phone down and turning to McTavish, Gary sighed, "Jesus, John, what am I going to do about that boy?"

John was John Louis McTavish—his English, French, and Scottish heritage all in plain sight through his names if not his tall WASPish appearance. Gary usually called him Professor, or as he liked to say, "Professker," just to wind him up. Whatever the pronunciation, the title was accurate, or it was until a year ago when an early retirement buyout from McTavish's mid-western state university allowed him to take up full-time residence in his cottage-in-progress on the coast of Maine.

In the time since, McTavish had worked at being an artist, worked on his cottage, worked for a few folks who needed some handyman help, and worked at what his late wife Maggie called his "abhorrent people skills." This last one grated a bit. McTavish knew she was right and he knew he could do better. Still, some part of him resisted any real change as most people left him cold.

It was an odd feeling, in a way, because McTavish quite enjoyed teaching. And he was good at it, at least in part, because he connected well with his students. He loved seeing their minds develop and deepen as they questioned each other, the texts they read, and even McTavish himself. Although he could be infinitely patient with his students, interacting deeply with other adults always seemed like too much bother. McTavish was honest enough with himself to know that he was making fewer gains on this project than on any of the others. But he counted Gary as a friend and, for now, McTavish would give himself a gold star in the friend department.

Looking at his friend, McTavish offered Gary the standard line, "Is there anything I can do?"

"Don't think so, Professker, unless you want to go sit with Ruby. She'll have her panties in a twist to be sure." He paused, and then said, "No, Julian will know what to do. The man's a true skunk, but he knows his stuff. If he could almost get that drifter Galen Knight off from underneath that murder charge, he ought to be able to get Jimmy out. Leastwise I hope so."

Always the realist, Gary knew Julian's failings as well as he did those of any other town resident. Julian was, Gary had concluded on more than one occasion, his own cat. Despite having lived in Rascal Harbor for nearly twenty years, Julian's "ways"—big city, snobbish, and cultured—still drew much attention, discussion, and derision among the locals. Until, of course, they needed his services. Then, that "son-of-a-bitch Julian" became *their* son-of-a-bitch.

Chapter 2

By contrast, no one had called McTavish a son-of-a-bitch, at least not since moving back to Maine or since the last time he had talked with his son.

Of course calling him a son-of-a-bitch would mean that Noah was actually talking to his father. And for now, he wasn't. Apparently there just weren't enough ways to apologize to a child for one's failings. The academic father trap—excessive pressure for scholarly achievements—might have been the primary source of trouble; maybe it was just a contributing factor along with a generally bad start. In any case, it was the cause to which Noah typically returned. McTavish honestly did not remember saying all that much, but whatever he had said, Noah read as parental disappointment. When he'd bring home report cards covered in Bs and Cs, McTavish tried to talk about the need to "reach one's potential" and the idea that "good grades mean good options." These and other sentiments were genuine and well-intentioned. To Noah's ears, however, they sounded like rebukes, especially when accompanied by what Maggie called, "That big sigh of yours."

"What sigh?" McTavish had asked the first time she made this claim, "I don't sigh. And I certainly don't have a *big* sigh."

"You do, even when you don't," Maggie said evenly. "And it's very demoralizing to Noah." McTavish couldn't say that he ever really knew what she was talking about—a sigh that's not a sigh? And a big sigh at that? But Maggie knew their lanky, troubled son in ways that continued to mystify her husband.

Maggie died the month before McTavish took the retirement. She'd beaten the skin and breast cancers that started in her late forties, but couldn't overcome the pancreatic variety discovered on her fiftieth birthday. McTavish knew that the valiance of her fight should have inspired him as it did so many of her friends. Cancer could not wipe the smile from her lips even if it could from her eyes. McTavish hated what that disease did to his wife, his best friend…and what it exposed in himself. Maggie's courage outdid his and it had taken McTavish a year, a retirement, and a move across the country to begin recovering. "Talking" with her daily, McTavish couldn't imagine a time when he didn't hear Maggie's voice.

Maggie and Noah defined McTavish's immediate family, but there were far more members in the larger McTavish clan. Scattered but deep, McTavish roots grew throughout Maine. Most of those roots grew on potato farms of the sort that used to feed and fund towns in the upper third of the state. Poor soil, poor crop yields, and poor investments eventually undercut this economic staple and today the family potato farm is more likely to show up on a farm store calendar than along Maine roadways. So while some McTavishes withered away in northern Maine towns, most sought lives elsewhere in the state. The fact that some of them left Maine altogether never set well with the many who didn't.

That split defined the McTavish siblings. Their parents, exhausted by a lifetime of work and children, died in the late '50s within months of one another. Their bond never faltered; their children's bonds never strengthened. With McTavish moving back, four of Malcolm and Nadine McTavish's five children now resided in Maine. Mark, Ruth, and Giselle lived inland, within an hour's drive from John and from one another. Daniel, the youngest, left for college in Chicago at eighteen and had found no reason to return. Mark and Ruth still blamed John for Danny's departure claiming that, as the oldest, it was his leaving that put the idea in Danny's head. That Danny was just as headstrong as his siblings seemed to be beside the point. In their view, Danny wouldn't have left if John hadn't. And so the McTavishes lived the life many parentless siblings do—they talked, argued, chattered behind each other's backs—though McTavish suspected that Mark and Ruth specialized here—visited infrequently, and lived their own lives.

Giselle lived closest to John in both physical and emotional proximity. After a dozen years of wandering through college campuses and course guides, Giselle and her friend Martin Mayberry settled fifteen miles north of John's cottage. Drawing on her interior design, business management, art history, and carpentry college courses, she'd found meaning in rehabbing old houses. Martin was equally talented as a plumber though, for some reason, Giselle always used a different plumber on her jobs. Their age difference aside, Giselle and John reached common ground around art, books, music, and wine. Everyone, John thought, ought to have a Giselle in their life.

Mark and Ruth—John couldn't think of one without thinking about the other—lived with their families in the same town some forty miles to the southwest. At fifty, Mark was but a few years younger than John, though he could have passed as the oldest sibling. John liked to think of himself as a fairly responsible adult. He had held a decent job, avoided jail, and voted more or less regularly. Mark did all of these things and more. He parlayed his associate's degree in business into a successful career in computer equipment sales. His territory covered all of New England, and his ego and belly seemed to grow every time he left the state. The McTavishes were generally a tall, slim-waisted group. Mark had always been the exception; the others joked that he must have eaten an unborn twin before birth. Ruth was as spare as Mark was round and their personalities followed their physiques. Mark's sunny disposition and quick laugh buoyed his deep-seated salesman's persona, though his wit could have a bite. Ruth, a bookkeeper, reversed Mark's ever-present grin. Ruth's comments, too, could sting, but she was generally quieter than her bigger brother. Both had married spouses of matching temperaments and produced off-spring similarly disposed.

The only light that ever seemed to shine in Mark's and Ruth's eyes came from three sources. One was the chance to skewer Giselle, who had always been an easy target. A dreamy kid, a dreamy college student, and a dreamy adult, Giselle finally found her niche in stripping old houses to their bones and putting them back together. Always of a practical mind, Mark and Ruth delighted in exposing Giselle's every last drift and dalliance. Doing so, John supposed, made them feel righteous about their single-minded pursuit of safety, security, and all things bland. They'd still prefer that Giselle get a real job, get married, and act a little more like them. Though less frequent now, their barbs still stung.

Mark's and Ruth's eyes also lit up when they could jab their brother, John. Now back home, he'd become their favorite object. John had enjoyed a career and a family and a house so, for a long time, Mark and Ruth confined their digs to the fact that John had left the state. "Oh, the prodigal son returns," one or the other would say within minutes every time Maggie, Noah, and John visited. "Don't look much like a Mainer anymore," Mark would say. "Doesn't sound much like one, either," Ruth would add. And so it went. There were hugs and cheek kisses for Maggie and Noah, and even some for John. But the ritual and vibe were always the same—"Don't think that you're anything special, Mister Indiana professor man."

Giselle always said that Mark and Ruth were actually proud of John and could be overheard to brag to neighbors whenever one of his books came out. "They've tried reading them," she said, "but the big words annoy them and that sort of sets 'em off again." She added, "But if they're chewing on you, then they're not chewing on me, and that's a good day in my book!"

"Well, enjoy it, little sister," John replied. "Mark and Ruth pride themselves on spreading their venom equally, so your turn will come back around."

One more source brought Mark and Ruth happiness—their brother Daniel. Although Mark and Ruth viewed John's life with mixed reactions, brother Daniel's was viewed as an unqualified success. "The boy's got the golden touch. It rains money all around him," Mark told anyone who would listen. "Lord, he sure does. If he ever fell in a pile of…well, you know…why he'd turn the smell into perfume!" Ruth said. The metaphors flowed freely when Danny was the conversational subject. They tended to mound up quickly, not unlike the shit pile Ruth wouldn't say; invariably Danny came out smelling like a rose. John didn't know if all the stories Danny told were true, but he was a charmer and a quick wit, and devilishly handsome. Danny traded well on these attributes, and John begrudged him no success. Moreover, John actually thought there was more substance to Danny than he sometimes wanted to let on. Where Mark and Ruth reveled in Danny's out-of-state success, John hoped he would move back to Maine as he thought he'd enjoy Danny's company.

Such were John McTavish's roots—and though some were tangled, gnarly, and strange, all ran deep in the rocky Maine soil. The McTavish family liked the saying that, while you can't choose your family, you can choose your friends…and you can always choose to shoot your family. McTavish actually believed his siblings loved one another, he just knew they didn't work very hard at it.

For better or worse, family defined a big part of McTavish's life; his work life, recently abandoned, also said a lot about the kind of man he was.

You couldn't grow up in Maine without an appreciation for history. You could hate the history of tough times, marginal existence, and the attendant traumas that came from a hard scrabble life, but you couldn't escape it. On the positive side was the fact that Mainers are inveterate storytellers. And their best stories always have a bit of evidence to support them, though that evidence can be hotly argued and sometimes violently contested. Stories-cum-history caused some of McTavish's old academic colleagues to sniff. As a professor, his specialty was the history of schooling, but he had always taken a broader view of the field: History was about why people do the things they do. Some of those things were noble, gracious, and bold; others were cowardly, venal, and pedestrian. All of it, McTavish thought, helped people think more and deeper about who they were, what they did, and how they might be better.

McTavish had loved the job. But then what's not to love about a career of reading, writing, and talking. Gary, and some of the boys who leaned against the walls of his shop, liked to scoff at McTavish's "Old cushy, yip-yap, Birkenstock" profession. McTavish would smile, nod in seeming agreement, and recall it fondly.

Now, however, McTavish was committed to his fledging career as an artist. He had always been good at stuff—not great at anything—but good at a lot of things. McTavish could write, do some plumbing, play a little guitar, and finish the Thursday crossword puzzle in the *New York Times*—the Friday through Sunday puzzles still made him feel like a dunce. McTavish was a better than average professor, and he hoped to become a better than average artist. Maggie's death had pushed him to realize that life was too short not to try. Once the home of Wyeth and Homer and Hopper, Maine had called McTavish back to his long-held cottage and the chance to craft a new life. He knew that Maggie would be jealous, but he knew she smiled at his return on the one hand and his venture outward on the other.

Retirement brings opportunity when it doesn't bring death. McTavish submitted his retirement papers and moved to Maine a month after Maggie's death. Their friends counseled against both moves. "You're still grieving, John," Maggie's friends had said. "This is not the time to make major life decisions." "What are you going to do, John?" McTavish's colleagues had said. "You're a professor, you've always been a professor. What are you going do in retirement?"

McTavish had smiled weakly, nodded, and murmured his way through these conversations. He knew they were right, but it didn't matter. He couldn't say which mattered more—the push to leave his

Indiana life or the pull to head east for a new one. It didn't matter. He drove to Maine.

McTavish had gone over to Gary's that morning to see if he wanted to join him in a cup of coffee to celebrate his three-month anniversary as a Rascal Harbor resident. He guessed it would have to wait.

CHAPTER 3

The rest of the day could hardly compete with McTavish's morning visit to Gary's. Afterward, he stopped at The Village Hardware to pick up some wire nuts and 14/2 cable and at Harbor Arts and Crafts for a new 3B pencil. The electrical parts were for an outlet his neighbor Miss Petrie asked him to replace. The pencil was necessary because McTavish had snapped his in half the previous night when he realized that his drawing of a man's hand wouldn't even get an honorable mention in a high school art contest.

McTavish had played with various media over the years—watercolor, oils, and pastels—and always with some success. But in starting his new life, he decided to go back to basics. The ability to draw well was central to good art, but drawing was vastly underrated as its own art form. Mark loved to chide McTavish about artists like Picasso saying, "How is that art? My kid could do that!" McTavish wanted to pull up images of the artist's drawings for they rivaled anything that the Renaissance masters had done. But Mark was no great fan of them either, saying, "Jesus, does everything they do have to be so dark? Can't they paint a sunny day?" Mark and Ruth favored the kind of art that arrived by the truckload, was sold in now empty mall store fronts, and matched the colors of the living room furniture.

Most folks thought of art only in its full-color representations—

Matisse's brightly colored primitives, Pollock's multi-colored drips, and Wyeth's muted color landscapes: It was color that ruled in the art world. McTavish appreciated well-rendered color in paintings, but he knew that, if he really wanted to understand and appreciate a piece and the artist who created it, he needed to see the drawings—those black and white bones that the artist later covered with color. McTavish suspected that someday he would return to using color—especially watercolor—but, for the time being, he wanted to see if he had what it took to produce great artistic drawings, whether in pencil, charcoal, or ink.

McTavish knew he was more productive when he had a couple of different projects underway. He focused on drawings of hands now—men's hands, women's hands, and children's hands; hands pointing, folded, praying, and working. Most people thought that faces were the toughest thing to draw, but hands had long interested and befuddled McTavish, and had required frequent trips to the art supply store for more pencils. To keep sane, McTavish interspersed his drawing sessions with carpentry, plumbing, and wiring in his cottage and for some of his neighbors. That day saw his pencils spared as he replaced the outlet for Miss Petrie's television.

It was nearly four PM when McTavish wrapped up for the day and began contemplating the evening's first dose of Bushmills Irish Whiskey. Before finishing a decent sketch of a hand in repose, he had gotten Miss Petrie and her television reacquainted—a good day's work and dramatic proof, he thought, of his Renaissance man qualities. McTavish did not get many calls—he had no land line or phone book listing—so he was startled when his mobile phone rang.

"John? You done for the day?" Gary said, his voice short. "I got a bottle of that fancy shit you drink and a clean…well, sorta clean…glass. If you got a minute, come on over."

So he did. "Fancy shit" was Gary's term for anything that wasn't Budweiser in a can. His bottle of Bushmills Irish would taste just as good as McTavish's own but he would have gone regardless. He was as curious about where things stood with Jimmy as he was about just how clean his glass would be.

McTavish drove his old Saab over to Gary's house on Widow's Way. Technically, Widow's Way is Willow's Way. But Randolph Beal, the town's long-dead maintenance man, thought of himself as something of a prankster. When the town voted to put up new street signage, Randolph decided to take a few liberties. He switched out a few letters on half a dozen of the town's street signs, "As a kind of a little joke," he explained once caught. Randolph died before he could redo all of his "jokes" and, by that time, his actions actually did seem kind of funny. So Willow's Way stayed Widow's Way as did the other creatively renamed signs for, to the town elders, it just seemed like too much bother to replace them.

As McTavish pulled into Gary's dooryard, he realized that he and Gary would not be alone. Ruby, Gary's very French wife, was likely to be there and was likely to be wound tight as a tick. Ruby loved her daughter, Louise. But Jimmy, or "Dimmy" in Ruby's odd locution, was her baby and, by every account, her favorite child. McTavish could only imagine how distraught Ruby would be.

But she wasn't. The news of Jimmy's arrest had reached her while Gary was on the phone with Julian. The mysterious, but highly effective grapevine that every small town cultivates had done its work. In this case, the grapevine came in the form of Mrs. Geneva Baxter who was much for gossip, but not much for facts. In her version of Jimmy's predicament, he was on his way to federal prison accused of theft, assault, and drug running. "Jimmy'll just never be able to shake this one off. That boy's going to the big house!" she had announced. Ruby might have calmed down on her own once Gary got home and adjusted Mrs. Baxter's report, but Ruby had found aid and support in the Manischewitz bottle readily available for occasions such as this.

Ruby wasn't completely in the bag when McTavish got there, but she would be soon. Gary's attempts to convince her to go lie down went nowhere. Ruby roamed the downstairs rooms, mug of wine in hand, while Gary and McTavish sat at the kitchen table.

After pouring a healthy measure of Bushmills into a semi-clean glass and popping the top on a can of Budweiser, Gary recounted the latest news. "Seems Jimmy was in the Portland jail because that's where he got picked up with the paintin'."

"He had it in hand?" McTavish asked incredulously.

"No. They found it in his trunk under an old tarp. Julian thinks they got some kind of tip that it was there, so it was an easy haul."

"A tit?" Ruby said in a slurred voice. "Dimmy's got a tit?"

Shaking his head, Gary said, "Jesus Christ, Ruby....It was a TIP, not a tit. Slosh some of that wine in your ears if you're gonna listen in."

"I suppose it was anonymous," McTavish said, trying to steer the conversation back to the story.

"Course it was, but how would the paintin' get there? I thought there were all kinds of people at that shindig the other night. Somebody would have seen him."

The shindig was the reception held at the Rascal Harbor Art Colony the night before. The star attraction had been a just-discovered Homer watercolor, and the local art world turned out in force to celebrate. The small piece, little bigger than a 3x5 index card, had been found in the attic of the Tillby place by their adult children. Mrs. Tillby had died a month earlier, and her husband followed her the day after his wife's funeral. "He died of a heart wreak," Ruby told McTavish at Mr. Tillby's funeral. Ruby could twist a metaphor like no one else McTavish had ever met, though this one took a little less time to untangle than most.

The Tillby's twin daughters returned to town to see to their mother's affairs and ended up seeing their father pass. Cleaning out the house was relatively easy. The elderly Tillbys lived meagerly on the first floor of their old Victorian. More crowded was the second floor and the attic, where Mrs. Tillby stacked her hoarded treasures forehead high. Most of the presumed treasures were just that, but the girls did find a box labeled, "The Good Stuff." Inside, they discovered an unsent love letter to John F. Kennedy from Mrs. Tillby, a modest-sized dime collection, a small Waterford vase with a nick in the rim, and a diminutive seascape with "Winslow Homer" lettered in the bottom right-hand corner. Although Homer's work has been forged regularly, the girls were not concerned. The Tillby family tree had had a branch that lived near Homer's studio in Prout's Neck. With enough social connections, the family made acquaintance with the artist and with enough money they had purchased a small watercolor.

Needless to say, the discovery set abuzz the small, but active art world in and around Rascal Harbor. "The Colony" wasn't one as such, but that's the name that the local arts council gave itself and the big, but crumbling building that housed its collection. Robertay Harding, matriarch of The Colony, convinced the Tillby girls to let the group host the unveiling of the Homer. Robertay could be nasty to those whose work she disliked—and even to some of those whose work she did. Still, the woman was a great organizer, and she put together a decent reception with the help of her on-and-off companion Thomas Beatty and the Art Colony board.

It was quite a shindig. Over 100 guests had arrived in everything from tuxedoes to tunics to T-shirts—the art crowd being known for its sartorial eclecticism. Most of the tuxedoes drove up from Portland and were equally split between Portland Museum of Art curators and art district gallery dealers. The tunics and T-shirts, some paint-splashed for effect, defined the range of outfits worn by the locals. Whatever the garb, festive greetings, air kisses, and calls for more wine filled the air. The reception was big-doings in Rascal Harbor, and the crowd was doing it up right.

Gary knew that McTavish had attended—in shirt, tie, and sports coat, all paint-free—so he quizzed him extensively, especially after McTavish said that he had seen Jimmy there.

"Well, what was the little Christer doin'?" asked Gary. "Did he look all shifty-eyed? Was he standin' around with the paintin' stickin' out of his pocket?" Gary was well into his third beer and though he was never much for finishing an "ing" ending, he dropped them continually now. Ruby, in a full Manischewitz mode, alternatively moaned Jimmy's name and what sounded like "Homey."

"He seemed normal enough to me," McTavish replied. "The place was packed, but I saw him talking to Bradley Little as Bradley stamped everyone's hand at the door. Later on, I saw Jimmy over near the bar, but I couldn't see who he was talking to."

"Probably talkin' with some art boy," Gary said, slurring his words. "Stupid fuckin' art."

"Art? Art who?" Ruby asked, coming out of her stupor for a minute. Gary didn't bother to answer, and Ruby went back to her moaning.

"If Bradley hadn't been at the door," Gary said, "I bet he woulda seen what happened…he woulda seen that Jimmy didn't do it." Catching a second wind, Gary moved on to the crime itself. "How the hell did that paintin' end up in Jimmy's trunk? And Christ, anyone coulda put it there. Jimmy's trunk's got a busted lock. It's just wired shut. Hell, anyone coulda undid the wire and put it in there."

It was hard to refute Gary's logic and McTavish told him so.

"Damn right, it coulda been anyone," Gary muttered as the beer muddled his thinking. "I just wisht Bradley was watching out for him."

"That Bradley," Ruby said, "he do anything for Dimmy."

The conversation stumbled along for a while longer, but few insights surfaced. McTavish learned that someone had tipped the Portland police as to Jimmy's crime. After conferring with their Rascal Harbor counterparts, they made the uncontested arrest. Gary added that Jimmy had been transported from Portland to the county jail, and that Julian was prepping for an arraignment the next day. Julian expected no problem in getting Jimmy out on bail, but Gary needed to organize his garage and house papers in order to meet the anticipated $50,000 surety. "I gotta get him outta there, John," Gary said. "Jail just ain't no place for a boy like Jimmy."

GEOFFREY SCOTT

McTavish stayed a while longer. Gary continued to drink and alternated between blaming Jimmy for being "an idiot" and wondering "how that boy is going to make it." Ruby stopped drinking because she kept dropping her mug. That didn't stop her, however, from making up rhymes about "Dimmy and Homey." At one point, Gary nodded toward Ruby, looked McTavish in the eye, and said, "Jesus, if she only knew."

Chapter 4

Many a Maine coastal town shared in the history of bootlegging. Like any social restriction, Prohibition limited the behaviors of some and liberated the behaviors of others. In this case, men…mostly…found ways to express their inclination to civil disobedience by moving liquor from distillery to customer in creative ways. Maine has some 3,500 miles of coastline, much of it hospitable to late-night landings. The aptly named Bureau of Prohibition, overwhelmed by the job of patrolling this stretch, largely ceded ground to the rum runners during the 1920s. Although they confiscated some 100 gallons of premium and less-than-premium hooch, far more passed them by. An estimated 1000 gallons found its way into Mainers' highball glasses, beer mugs, and wine goblets.

Rascal Harbor, once known as Willmont, gained its name from one of the more successful Bureau intercessions. In 1925, agents captured a large fishing boat loaded hard with a cargo of Jamaican rum, English gin, and Southern moonshine. Tipped off to the shipment, twenty Bureau agents quickly identified the boat for the bootlegger that it was. Running with no lights and about a foot of freeboard, and running only fast enough to stay ahead of the biggest swells, the *Jasper* presented an easy catch. The crew of stout Maine men thought about resisting, but the sight of Tommy guns and a gathering sea convinced them otherwise. "We got the rascals," Lester Dodge, the lead agent in the case, said proudly. Little did he know, however, that the local lads had landed a shipment twice that size only three days earlier. Still, the biggest bootlegging bust at the time got much media attention. Agent Dodge, apparently one to seize on a word and not let go, kept talking about the "rascals" he and his men had captured. The term stuck—both with the lawless and the law-abiding—and, after a couple of years, a sign welcoming tourists to "Rascal Harbor" covered the old Willmont one. Town crews removed the sign only to see a new one appear. Eventually the town fathers acceded to the inevitable and petitioned the state for a change of name. It's not clear if the petition was ever approved, but the petitioners would not be denied. Willmont became Rascal Harbor and soon the tourist trade brought in far more revenue than illicit liquor ever had.

The tourist trade and legal liquor continued to go hand in hand to support the Rascal Harbor economy. The sea still provided, but what it provided *now* was considerably different than it had in the past.

Commercial fishing paid some of the bills. Fishing was a generic term, though, as it obscured the variation in the types and sizes of boats, the equipment they carried, and the species the fishermen pursued. Lobstermen generally worked by themselves or with a sternman—the term applied to either gender. In their small to medium-sized boats, they used powerful winches to haul traps from the ocean floor. Fishing for scallops and shrimp called for more workers, larger boats, and the use of nets and booms. Scallops lived on the sea bed, so were fished with dredge nets; shrimp swam, however, so trawl nets were set just above the ocean floor. Fishermen caught flounder and haddock in nets, which were set even further off the ocean bottom, but they also caught them on longlines. Long line fishing was just what the name says— long lines of heavy filament with hooks attached at various intervals.

Tuna, sharks, and swordfish were predominantly caught on long lines.

Fishing the Maine coast was still profitable, though overfishing, climate change, and other challenges had cut the commercial fleet nearly in half since the mid-1990s. Working harbors drew tourists, artists, and photographers, but most of the hard, physical, and dangerous work of fishing was done at sea rather than at the docks. And the big money now chased the "touristas" harder than it did the fish.

Tourism ruled the Maine economy now. Hotels, restaurants, bars, and stores competed for tourist dollars and for the lowest wages. In coastal towns like Rascal Harbor, those wages could be higher than in northern Maine, especially in the heat of the summer when the labor supply was short. High living costs, however, crimped any real opportunities for most coastal workers to live the high life. There was money to be made, but the inequities of income distribution were no different in the tourist trade than they were or had been in any other industry.

And yet, it was quite easy to think happier thoughts on a summer day seated on a restaurant deck eating a lobster roll and drinking a locally-made craft beer. Social stagnation, income inequalities, struggling schools, and a winter that was longer than it needed to be by half were all important issues. But when the sun shone and a mild ocean breeze kicked up, it was hard to find a finer place on earth.

Geography had blessed Rascal Harbor. A wide harbor with deep water allowed the biggest commercial boats and the beamiest pleasure craft ample space to moor or dock. Numerous coves, inlets, and bays surround the harbor, offering more dockage and more real estate on which to build seaside dwellings. The roads that connected the Harbor and its enclaves varied in size, but tended toward the narrow, which meant that drivers had to exercise a degree of self-control in order to avoid a trip to the auto body shop.

The town of Rascal Harbor proper followed the contours of the harbor with a mix of retail stores, dining and hospitality establishments, single and multi-family residences, public buildings, and the businesses that serviced the year-round and summer populations' needs. Once, those businesses consisted of places to get your hair cut, your car repaired, and your taxes done. Today, they included day spas, investment counseling centers, nail and tanning salons, and tattoo parlors, though the last were a far cry from the stereotype. The town terrain rose up around the harbor such that most of the Harbor buildings laid at more than one level and a simple tour of the town strained the calf muscles and lung capacity of many visitors.

Route 17, the single road leading down to the Harbor from Route 1, was heavily traveled during the summer; making a turn across the traffic flow could sometimes take as long as ten minutes. During the winter, the traffic problems faded, but sleet and freezing rain made the drive just as troublesome.

Driving down the last hill and arriving in the Harbor invariably brought a smile. "Quaint" only began to describe the natural beauty of the harbor and hills. And the man-made intrusions reflected a kind of simplicity and charm that defined small-town, oceanside Maine.

The houses and stores in and around the town were classic New England—white-clapboard Victorians, gray-shingled cottages, red-brick storefronts—all built close to the sidewalks. Trim work could take any number of hues, but tended toward whites, blues, and greens. Hand-carved signs predominated and shamed the few neon and plastic ones in evidence. A lived-in, and worked-in, quality enveloped the town. But rather than portraying the run-down grime of a Maine factory town, Rascal Harbor felt like a place where people had lived, worked, and died since humans realized the power of the sea. The ugliness that reflected a larger culture more attentive to gloss than to authenticity was there, but it tended to be more obvious on the outer stretches of Route 17 than in the Harbor proper.

A coastal Maine town was more than economics and geography, but these forces mattered in no small way. Each offered opportunities and constraints, prospects and problems. What the Rascal Harbor residents did with what they had also mattered in no small way.

Chapter 5

The theft of the Homer painting put Rascal Harbor on the front page of the state newspapers and in the first ten minutes of every Maine TV news broadcast. It even garnered a brief mention in several national outlets. Predictably, the attention focused on the lax security surrounding the event—apparently checking a guest list and stamping the invitees' hands with ink left something to be desired as a protective measure.

Robertay Harding fumed about the audacity of someone disrupting her carefully prepared event and about the varied spelling and pronunciation that her self-created name received in the media. Jimmy's friend, Bradley Little, who had volunteered to stamp the hands, shrugged and smiled when interviewed by reporters. The other attendees expressed the typical array of shock, outrage, and concern about the continued safety of the masterwork. Under the assumption that any press is good press, the town fathers secretly rejoiced that news of the crime would incite an even bigger tourist crowd next summer.

Despite the presence of over 100 guests, little about the theft could be discerned from their observations. The evening went well for the most part—patrons gushed over the Homer, nodded toward some Colony artists' work, and snickered over still other pieces. The wine and conversation flowed freely as guests chattered about the likelihood of more unfound works, the price this piece would fetch, the relative value of Homer and other American artists, and whose outfit looked the most pretentious.

McTavish didn't see what happened, but a minor fracas developed when one tippled guest collided with another close enough to bump the stand on which the Homer was displayed and send it wafting to the floor. Robertay had decided that the painting would not be permanently mounted, but rather affixed to a large board with an apparently flimsy adhesive. So when the stand tipped over, the watercolor fluttered downward. Order and the painting were quickly restored with Jimmy, Bradley, and a few others jumping in to save the painting from being trodden. Robertay seized control of the moment, quieting the crowd and announcing that the Homer was "Made of good, solid Maine stock, just like everyone here!" Cheers erupted, smiles returned, and wine flowed.

After a gala evening, the news that the painting had been stolen and that the culprit was one of Rascal Harbor's own shocked all. The news reporters of both print and broadcast exercised a fair amount of discretion in describing Jimmy's involvement. They noted his arrest and the circumstances of the painting's discovery. None mentioned the broken trunk latch as that detail was withheld from the public police report. Much was made, however, of Jimmy's status as a poor college art student with a run-down car and a low-rent flop. No one really knew what an art thief was supposed to look like, but Jimmy's fair profile and model-thin body seemed to fit the role. That the boy could use the money from a back alley sale seemed almost too obvious to mention.

And so the town wags had fresh meat. Jimmy heard none of the talk as it took a good part of the next day to free him on bond. Ruby also heard little as her wine-laden brain dulled her to the doorbell and telephone. Gary, however, was fair game as friend and foe pounced.

It was Jimmy, however, who showed up on McTavish's doorstep that evening. Though it was only seven PM, by that point in the fall, darkness and a chill arrived together. Jimmy, wearing one of his father's barn coats and a weathered baseball cap, knocked and entered McTavish's kitchen. Though the cottage itself wasn't large, the kitchen was. In addition to an aged wooden table, two rocking chairs welcomed guests to sit and talk in the warm kitchen light. McTavish and Jimmy settled into the chairs after Jimmy removed the coat and hat.

"How do you like my disguise?" he asked. As soon as he said it, McTavish realized that Jimmy would never have worn these garments under normal circumstances. "It was Mom's idea," Jimmy continued. "She wanted me to stay home, but I told her I needed to see you. She thought I'd get hassled if I went out in my regular clothes, so she dressed me up like dad."

"Not much of a disguise," McTavish said. "You're 30 pounds lighter and three inches taller than your father. Plus you've got that red bandana tied around your neck."

"Ah, shit." Although the boy tried to clean up his language around McTavish, the obscenity gene so apparent in his father could not be easily erased. "Mom was right. She said dad wouldn't wear it. Guess I should have honked my nose on it and left it sticking out of my back pocket."

McTavish let Jimmy and Ruby's attempt at disguise pass and pushed on to see how the boy was doing.

"I'm just okay," Jimmy muttered. "Feels like I'm caught in one of those Escher drawings, though—stairs leading here and there, walls all around, none of it making any sense."

Though McTavish suspected the boy had recounted the story many times already, he asked, "Do you want to talk it through or would you rather talk about art?"

"I'd love to talk about art, but there may not be much in my future if I can't get out from under this crime. Jesus, John, they're talking about locking me up for ten years!" The strain in the boy's face and voice, invisible up to this point, suddenly broke through. He cried softly, shoulders shaking. McTavish, never much for emotion, rocked silently beside him.

A couple of minutes later, Jimmy regrouped, blew his nose, and looked at McTavish with wounded puppy eyes. "Let's talk about it," he said. "Maybe you can help me sort it through. Mom certainly couldn't. She asks a question, starts crying, stops, asks a different question, and cries again. And dad…I guess I just feel the worse for him. He walks around swearing under his breath, but he won't even look at me. I don't know if he's ashamed of me or scared for me or mad at me…." New tears ran down Jimmy's cheeks. He pushed on, though, and McTavish couldn't help but admire the boy.

"It's just that I can't imagine how that painting got in my trunk. Who would put it there and why? What's anyone got against me?"

"Can you not think of anyone who would do you harm?"

"I really can't. This is a nightmare."

McTavish couldn't argue the point, so he said, "So, let's talk it all through." McTavish had put the coffee pot on and, before Jimmy started his narrative, McTavish poured the first of what he expected would be several mugsful of the brew.

"So you know that Robertay asked me to attend," Jimmy said. "She said she wanted to lower the average age of the guests by inviting me and some other younger artists."

"But Bradley isn't an artist." McTavish knew that Bradley was Jimmy's good friend, but that he had no interest in art.

"No, Robertay rounded up a bunch of kids to help out during the event. Bradley volunteered to do the hand stamping at the door," Jimmy said. "Tommy Draper was working at the bar. Mindy Jones and another girl passed around food."

"Could any of them have stolen the painting?"

"Christ, no. I've never had any problem with any of them, and Bradley's been as close to a best friend as I've ever had."

"Did you know many of the other artists?" McTavish asked. "Hard to believe an out-of-towner would try to frame you."

"Well, I knew most of the Colony folks. I've been hanging around trying to get them to look at my work for years. Simon, Jona, Toni, you know, all the regulars. Some of 'em have been really helpful to me—even giving me free lessons at times. They've all got their quirks, some serious quirks, but I can't imagine any of them would be gunning for me."

McTavish snapped his fingers. "What if it *was* an out-of-towner? What if one of the Portland crowd stole the painting, panicked, and then hid it in your trunk?" McTavish smiled inwardly at his own cleverness.

"Maybe." Jimmy didn't seem convinced. "Dad wired up my trunk latch when it broke and he didn't have the right part to fix it." After a pause, he said, "I suppose one them could have done it."

"Was there anyone else there? Anyone who wasn't a local artist, a local kid, or a Portland dealer?"

"Yup." Jimmy stood and retrieved the coffee pot to refill their mugs. "I mean, you were there. All kinds of town folks came—the town manager, some of the selectmen, you know, the folks who show up just to show up."

McTavish knew well what the boy meant. Some prominent Rascal Harbor residents would attend any Colony event even though they wouldn't know a watercolor from a water closet. Free booze and food guaranteed a crowd.

"Jesus, what a mess," McTavish said. "That's a lot of people to account for." After a minute, he continued, "Well, let's take it from another angle. If we can't make any headway on the people, let's talk through the event."

For the next twenty minutes, Jimmy and McTavish traded accounts of what they had seen, heard, and thought during the reception. Both began the night by getting their hands stamped by Bradley, who seemed more excited by the job than either could imagine. Both also saw that, while the Homer watercolor got close attention from most of the crowd as they entered, the free wine and the chance to hobnob seemed almost as popular.

Their recollections differed around the jostling of the painting. Jimmy saw Marie Townsend, a selectman, teeter by, bump a man Jimmy assumed to be a Portland art dealer, who then knocked the artwork to the floor. According to Jimmy, Marie's teetering resulted from "Those hideous, four-inch, yellow heels" worn on feet more used to deck shoes. McTavish had also seen people, including Marie, bumping one another close to the Homer. But he'd also seen Marie visit the bar enough times to suspect that inebriation might be as much to blame as her footwear for the ensuing melee. Recollections of those involved in the scrum varied considerably. Though both saw people they didn't know, Jimmy recalled seeing Art Colony board members Simon Britton and Jona Lewis trying to help, while McTavish saw another artist, Toni Ludlow, and police chief Lawton Miles. McTavish said he also thought he saw Nellie Hildreth, editor of the weekly *Rascal Harbor Gazette*, get pushed aside.

At the mention of Nellie, Jimmy said, "Jesus, John, did you see the obituary Nellie wrote for Truman Landis in last week's paper? Mom was reading it to me the other day. It's a classic."

"Nope, must have missed it."

Jimmy picked up the paper lying on top of a pile of art books. He thumbed through to the obituaries and began to read:

Truman Landis, 75, of Rascal Harbor, died at home all by his lonesome on October 1. Truman was a lobsterman of some renown, but not much of a human being. He died alone because he wasn't on speaking terms with half the townsfolk, having sworn at, sued, or tried to run over most of them. A generous interpretation would say that Truman had just a little *too* much character. A less generous one would say he was a pisspot. Truman was pre-deceased by his brother Lawrence and a sister, Rachel, both of whom thought Truman was just a little too special for his own good. Services will be held at the Rascal Harbor Methodist Church, where Truman was a sometime participant. Flowers are welcome, but not expected.

"And that's one of the nicer ones," Jimmy said. "Mom remembers one where Nellie said the lady was a 'woman of the early evening.' How can she get away with that?"

GEOFFREY SCOTT

"Apparently, Nellie makes it clear that the relatives can offer some text for their beloved, but she reserves the right to 'enhance' it for the readership. She'll take what they wrote, but she knows everyone and everything, and so feels it only right that she 'revise as needed.'"

"Christ. Small towns."

Both men nodded and continued rocking.

"So, do you have a theory?" McTavish asked.

"Wish I did. Wish there was something I could offer Chief Miles to get him off my ass. Not sure what I ever did to him, but he just seems to have it in for me."

"Lawton hates anyone who is different," McTavish said. "He'll go to the Colony events, but mostly just to see what kind of deviance is developing and consider ways that he might root it out. He's not a man to cross."

"I don't think I ever did, but he seems to think the worst of me. He actually spoke out against me getting bail today."

Sensing that there was no more progress to make that evening, Jimmy said his goodbyes, leaving McTavish to wonder how his young friend would fare over the coming weeks and months. McTavish had no doubt that Chief Miles hated homosexuals. Jimmy had not opened up about his sexuality, but McTavish knew that it was a topic of conversation among the town folk. Gary was a long-time local, and generally well-liked. That didn't prevent those who knew him, and even some of his so-called friends, from asking, "How the hell could that boy have come from Gary Park?" McTavish knew that Gary loved his son, but he also knew that he loved his son Noah. And sometimes love just wasn't enough.

CHAPTER 6

Although Jimmy and McTavish had exhausted themselves trying to solve the mystery, the rest of Rascal Harbor pushed on. A major crime was not an everyday occurrence in small Maine towns. When it happened, it consumed all the oxygen in the air.

Like many coastal towns discovered by the tourist trade—"summer pukes," as Gary called them—restaurants and diners, bars and ice cream shops competed for vacationers' dollars. Many did so well that their owners could work the seven months from Memorial Day to Columbus Day, and then winter on a beach in Florida. Others, like Lydia's Diner, stayed open year round. They got their share of tourist dollars, but they preferred to take a slower route to their fortunes.

Trudy Turner, whose small frame carried just enough extra weight to annoy her, was the owner of Lydia's and the daughter of its founder. Trudy tolerated the tourists, but she loved the locals—most of them anyway.

Each morning a crew of retired fishermen, men who had ceded the sea to their sons and grandsons, occupied the scarred, rectangular table in the back left corner of the diner. At a similarly constructed table on the right sat an array of similarly aged women, most of whom had spent more time managing kids and bills and jobs than their 401k funds. The men typically arrived in well-aged flannel shirts and saggy blue jeans, the only concession to the cooler temps being the occasional quilted vest. The ladies dressed much the same, though a chambray shirt and a fleece jacket could be substituted at times. The short hallway to Lydia's kitchen separated the two groups and, for the most part, they held court in parallel fashion. On occasion, however, the two groups would mix it up.

The front of Lydia's was brightly lit, though the lighting fixtures seemed to be purposefully chosen to be at odds with one another. Fluorescent tube, single bulb, and recessed lights somehow combined to offer an inviting glow. That glow spread across the soft yellow walls that sported an equally eclectic array of every knick and knack one could imagine. "Early attic," Trudy had explained to a tourist who had the nerve to ask what her décor schema was. "Folks bring in shit they don't want any more and, if they can find a spot, they put it up," Trudy said.

The morning after the news of the theft broke, Maude Anderson, a short, plump woman, broached the topic once the girls had assembled. "By gorry, can you believe Jimmy Park's been arrested down Portland way for stealing that paintin'?"

The previous day's conversation had covered the high price of scallops, the low state of the Red Sox, and what the town mill rate might be that year. This morning, however, no secondary topics surfaced. It would be all Jimmy Park, all the time.

"Well, that's what they're sayin'," June Pickering said. "Hard to know what the real story might be." June and Maude were the same height, but June's body carried far less padding.

"Ayuh," said Geraldine Smythe, a tall, solid woman who invariably wore a brightly colored scarf tied at the neck. She added, "But that's not stopping Geneva from spreading stories all over town. She had Ruby in a fisherman's knot yesterday with her nonsense." All shook their heads at the mention of Geneva Baxter. Geneva seemed a kind and sensible spirit until she opened her mouth. Always the first to hear any good gossip in the town, Geneva was the worst at getting the facts in order.

"Geneva don't know her ass from a hole in the ground," added Minerva Williams, a rangy woman of medium height. "If she ever saw a fact, she'd wrassle it to the ground, spit in its face, and call its mother a whore!" Some cheeks colored at Minerva's profanity but, truth be told, none disagreed with the characterization. Once considered an eccentric, Geneva now seemed a genuine nuisance. The ladies liked their *news*—none would call it gossip—but they wanted it straight. Geneva's embellished versions offended them mightily.

"You might well be right about that," Geraldine said. "Still, the boy's in a tight spot, dontcha know."

"*If* he did it," argued Karen Tompkins, who bucked the trend of flannel and jeans in favor of berry-colored track suits. "Jimmy Parks is not stupid. If he did steal the painting, he'd never have put it in his trunk under an old tarp. I've heard him talk about Winslow Homer like the old guy was a god. I suppose he'd love to have one of Homer's paintings, but he wouldn't treat it that way."

Karen's logic settled the conversation for a few minutes as each of the ladies weighed its merits. They knew Jimmy to be a fastidious and clean boy, and probably gay. Every one of them had seen Jimmy working at his father's garage where he changed oil, checked timing belts, and corrected the alignment of their cars…and then meticulously clean his hands and nails. Karen's observation boosted their collective inclination to trust the boy's innocence.

"Hmmm. Karen's got a good point. But if she's right, then it's got to be a frame-up. And who would want to frame Jimmy?" Geraldine asked.

Geraldine's question set the girls' minds reeling, and they tripped over each other to offer conjectures.

"I bet it was one of them Portland folks," suggested Maude.

"Maybe, but I'd lay odds on Chief Miles," said June. "That man's always had a flinty eye out for anyone who's different."

"Hell, it could be any one of those artsy-fartsy assholes," said Minerva. "Christ, I wouldn't put it passed Robertayyyy." She drew out the last syllable and caused her friends to giggle. "That woman is a right nightmare, and look at all the publicity she and the Colony are gettin'!"

June made a dismissive sound. "She likes the publicity, I'll grant you that, but she likes Jimmy, too. She thinks he's got real talent."

"Maybe so, but I wouldn't put it past the bitch to wrangle up a mess like this just to get her ugly old mug on the news," Minerva said.

Robertay Harding had lived in Rascal Harbor for nearly 30 years, but would always be considered an outsider. She'd never lost her New York accent nor her propensity to treat the locals in a slightly condescending fashion. Sure, she worked with her hands, but brushing paint on a canvas was far different work than picking crabmeat, shucking oysters, or slinging food in the school cafeteria. Robertay had irritated the ladies from day one. They might have embraced her at some point, but she'd given them no reason to try.

Robertay was often the topic of conversation at the men's table as well, though it was the size of her breasts more than her New York City ways that piqued their interest. "Christ, did you see Robertay's boobs on the TV last night?" asked Vance Edwards. "Those puppies were barkin' for attention!" Edwards was a muscular man of medium height. Unlike any of his friends, Vance arrived each morning in wife-pressed jeans and shirts. The shit he'd taken for doing so had largely worn off.

"You ain't wrong about that," Bill Candlewith said. "Those things deserve their own zip codes." A short, wiry man, Candlewith limped due to a fishing boat accident.

"Well, while you mutts were here ogling Robertay's triple Zs, I was listening to the actual report," said Rob Pownall, a tall man with a weathered face and weathered clothes to match. "Jimmy Park is in serious trouble."

"No shit, Sherlock, " said Caleb Rimes, a thick-barreled man who reveled in being known as a slob. Younger than the other back table men, Caleb was only a regular when he wasn't working; he often wasn't working. "I heard that paintin' is worth a million bucks. That ain't no misdemeanor he's accused of. The little fag could be behind bars with all the other boys for a long, long time."

"Cut it out, Caleb," said Rob. "Whether the boy's a gay or not has nothing to do with whether he stole the painting."

"Course it doesn't," Caleb said, pushing forward. "But that goddamn art crowd all think they can do whatever the hell they want to without consequence one."

"Actually, that sounds a lot like you," Ray Manley said. Manley was the oldest of the men and his bent body reflected years of heavy toil. Ray was the most likely of the men to need an over shirt or vest in the coming fall as his spare body could hold no heat. "Hell, Caleb, you never take responsibility for anything you do," Ray added. "Remember that time you got caught speedin' and you told the cop that he had no right to arrest you because it was 'a man's nature to seek out speed'?"

"What was that last part, Ray?" Slow Johnston asked. Slow, whose real name was Samson, was always late to the morning table. Lydia's tables could barely accommodate five beefy men so one man, usually Slow, had to sit slightly outside the group. The other men were sizable; Slow was a giant. His outsized head, hands, and trunk challenged the fit of any clothing item and his knees, elbows, and belly popped through most everything he wore. The hearing in Slow's right ear had suffered when he was hit in the head by a lobster trap that he'd pulled up too fast. For some unknown reason, he always turned that ear toward the conversation and, consequently, heard even less than he would have normally.

"For Christ's sake, Slow, turn your good ear toward the table," said Vance.

"Oh, right," said Slow, who promptly forgot that he'd neither heard nor understood Ray's last point.

The conversation ambled on over a second cup of coffee. Julia Nisbett, Lydia's efficient and only waitress, limited the boys to two cups each. A thin woman, but one with sinewy muscles in her arms and legs, Julia seemed to burn calories faster than she could ingest them.

"If I didn't limit those boys, I'd hafta make another po[t] would chew through that one, too. I can only listen to thei[r] long!" Julia explained to the ladies across the hallway. The ladies, of whose daughters Julia had gone to school with, could have gotte[n] a third cup, but all had work and social obligations and so seldom lingered. Julia kept track of the coffee as well as the conversations and, on that morning, she realized that she didn't know a thing more than she had when her shift had started. "Yak, yak, sip, sip," she said to Trudy. "Another day in Gossip Town."

CHAPTER 7

While Lydia's patrons dissected what was known about the case on the street, the Rascal Harbor police had been pursuing the matter behind the scenes. Leading the effort was Dick Chambers, Rascal Harbor's chief—and only—detective. After taking a bullet five years earlier, Chambers had taken early retirement from the police force of a sprawling south Florida city. Chambers's partner had botched his part of a drug raid and Chambers paid the price. Though not life threatening, the wound inspired a round of personal and career reflection. Once healed, Chambers turned north to the state his Maine-born mother always praised. He took his small pension, his medium-sized injury settlement, and his big dream of life in a cooler climate and settled in Rascal Harbor.

With plenty of policing experience and at a tall and fit fifty years of age, Chambers seemed everything that his boss was not. Chief Lawton Miles maintained the department's books, smiled at civic events, and handled the politics of a town of 2500 year-round residents and 150,000 summer complaints. What he lacked in policing knowledge and skills, he made up for in administrative cunning. The police budget never got cut, always had money for uniform updates, and supported Chief Miles's small, but cozy waterfront home. Detective Chambers knew Miles to be a first-rate ass and suck-up, but he had no interest in

GEOFFREY SCOTT

38

the chief's job. He just hoped that he'd be able to retire before he got fired for punching his boss in the face.

Chambers, with the assistance of the department sergeant Andy Levesque, had spent two days doing face-to-face and telephone interviews with the Homer reception guests. As always, he was amazed at the weak coherence of their collective memories. Most remembered the kerfuffle with the bumped painting and the relatively poor quality of the wine. Little else gelled, however. Chambers's notes showed upwards of five different people jarring the easel where the painting was displayed and another ten involved in the struggle to pick it up. No consensus surfaced around a motive or a culprit.

Jimmy Park's interview went about as expected: He said nothing. Before the interview, Jimmy pleaded with his lawyer to tell his story to the police. Julian Pratt's admonition that he keep quiet was reinforced by Gary. "Just shut your trap, boy," he had said. "If they got anything for sure, then let 'em bring it forward. But Miles is just looking to pin this thing on you and he'll twist whatever you say to prove it." Julian might have dressed up this lecture in prettier language, but he could not argue with Gary's logic. Both men had grudging respect for Detective Chambers; neither trusted Chambers's boss.

The evidence against Jimmy damned him—after all, the painting was in the trunk of his car. The fact that the trunk could have been accessed by anyone, the fact that Jimmy's fingerprints did not appear on the painting, and the fact that Jimmy was a smart kid who would have realized the idiocy of the act bothered Detective Chambers. Such facts bothered Chief Miles not at all and he oddly pressed Chambers to "Find the smoking gun."

Though it wasn't a gun, the discovery of a key to the back door of the Art Colony gallery seemed like a big break.

Detective Chambers had just finished another frustrating attempt to get Jimmy Park's side of the story, when Artie Long, one of the two department constables, burst into the interview room. "You gotta come, sir!" Artie called, cutting his eyes toward Jimmy. "We got somethin'."

After his own long look at Jimmy, Chambers muttered, "Might as well. I'm not getting anywhere in here."

"Always happy to help, Detective Chambers!" Julian chided, though silently he worried about what the discovery might be. He knew it was foolish, but he actually believed in Jimmy's innocence. The boy had certainly pushed that position hard enough. But Julian couldn't count how many times he had heard "I'm innocent!" only to learn the opposite soon afterward. He'd heard his clients' protestations of a system gone bad, an in-law frame-up, or a wrong place/wrong time snafu. He typically listened patiently with a face that registered both interest and resignation. This time his head and his gut told him that Jimmy Park was innocent. Still, Julian worried. Something might have turned up linking Jimmy to the theft. Whether that something was legitimate or planted, however, added to his worries.

The key had been missed on the first two searches. Detective Chambers always demanded that multiple inspections be conducted of crime scenes. He had had too many cases come together after a second or third search yielded evidence missed earlier to stop the practice now. In this case, he sensed that nothing else would be gained after the first two explorations proved fruitless. Then he heard Rendall Kalin's voice.

Rendall Kalin, the other Rascal Harbor constable, annoyed Chambers. Although everyone in town knew Kalin would be a constable for life, he fancied himself next in line for Chambers's job. He read mysteries, watched crime shows, and had done reasonably well in the basic training course he had taken to become a Law Enforcement Officer. Kalin parlayed this knowledge and experience into endless discourses about the minds, habits, and behaviors of criminals and the circumstances, personalities, and evidence that emerged in investigations. Overhearing Kalin offer his latest conjecture on why "It's just got to be the Park kid" earlier that day, Chambers had ordered him to do another sweep of the Colony gallery site.

"In my considered opinion, Detective Chambers, little would be gained—"

"Get your big ass and your considered opinion out there and research the area."

"Aye, aye, skipper," Kalin said, a bit too loudly. With a mock salute, he turned and headed to his cruiser.

Chambers expected Kalin to spend the rest of the day at the Colony site…or dubbing around getting over there and back. So as he walked into the department lobby with Constable Long, Chambers was surprised to see Kalin with chest thrown out and smile a'beaming.

"I found the key to the Colony, and it's right here, Detective Chambers," Kalin said, patting his pants pocket. "It's the key to the crime! Get it? The KEY to the crime?"

"Yeah, yeah, Kalin, out with it," Chambers said.

Through his broad grin, Constable Kalin began taking the assembled group through his search beginning with his drive to the gallery. "Jesus, just get to it, Rendall," Chambers said as calmly as he could.

"Right, right, detective," Kalin replied. "So I was conducting a close perimeter search of the building in question, when all of sudden I see a twinkle right underneath siding. 'What's that?' I asked myself, 'could it be a clue?'" Kalin paused, presumably for dramatic effect. As he saw Chambers's face color, he continued. "Well, sir, I got down on my knees, poked around, and came up with this key, right there by the back door to the gallery. So I tried it in the door and, well, you can guess the rest. She opened up just like my first girlfriend!"

"Gross," mumbled Gabby Angler, the department secretary and dispatcher.

"That's enough of that," added Sergeant Levesque, anticipating Chambers's reaction.

"Right, right," Kalin said. "Well, anyway, the key fit the door and so I raced right back to the station."

"Let's see it," Chambers said.

Kalin reached into his pants pocket and withdrew a silver key in a plastic evidence bag. As he started to hand it to the detective, Kalin stopped and said, "Well, you might find my fingerprints on it…"

STEALING HOMER

Flinching, as if anticipating Chamber's pounce, Kalin rushed on. "You gotta understand, Detective, I was finishing up my search when I see the twinkle. I guess the sun musta caught it just right and, well, I guess I got excited and forgot to put on a glove or get a stick or something. I just kinda reached in there and pulled it out. And then when I see that it's a key, right there by the back door, well sir, I jumped up, tried it in the door, and she opened right up just like—"

"Yeah, we know," Chambers said. "So a good lead is now compromised because we've got your fingerprints all over it. Any other prints are likely obliterated or smudged." Chambers stopped as the constable seemed about to deflate. Though he wasn't sure it would do any good, he knew there would be time to school the boy about evidence retrieval later on. For now, he just hoped Kalin hadn't screwed up the only real clue they had. "Bittersweet, Kalin," he said. "Good find. Not so great follow-up, but a good find." He handed the bagged key to Sergeant Levesque and asked him to get it processed.

As everyone returned to their desks, Julian turned to Jimmy, raised an eyebrow, and put his finger to his lips.

Chapter 8

No news is boring news in small towns. Discovery of the gallery key induced new interest in and a raft of new theories about the Homer theft. Tongues wagged at Harbor Hair and at Harbor Arts and Crafts, at Village Hardware and Village Pizza, and at Robertay and Thomas's cottage, at Gary and Ruby's house, and at Nellie Hildreth's office at the *Gazette*. Although Detective Chambers hoped to keep the news of the key quiet until he could learn to whom it belonged, he wasn't surprised to learn of its leak.

It was also no surprise that the news got its biggest airing at Lydia's Diner. With the tourists mostly gone, tables filled with locals and the two tables in the back filled nearly as soon as Trudy unlocked the door. The fact that the only real revelation was that a key had been found inhibited the conversations not one bit.

"What will that key mean to the investigation?" asked June Pickering as soon as her tablemates settled into their coffee cups.

"I wouldn'ta thought Robertay would allow anyone else to have a key," Maude Anderson said. "She keeps a pretty tight handle on the Colony."

"That's not the only thing that bitch keeps tight," Minerva Williams said in a booming voice. "Thomas B. has got to be one frustrated old dog."

"Easy, Minerva," Geraldine Smythe said. "You don't know. Robertay could be a regular mattress tiger."

"Girls, really!" June admonished.

"Hell, Junie, you know it's true," Minerva said. "She's got them big old boobs, but I bet Thomas only sees 'em in his dreams!"

June shook her head, reddened, and giggled.

"Let's get back to the issue at hand," Karen Tompkins said. "If it wasn't Robertay's key, and I think we can be fairly sure it isn't, then who does it belong to? Would Jimmy have one?"

"Doesn't seem likely," Geraldine said. "Jimmy's not one of the gray heads. My bet is that it belongs to one of the Colony board or whatever they call themselves. They're the only ones I think Robertay would give keys to."

"Makes sense," Karen said in agreement. Most of the others nodded as well. "But who's on the board?"

"Don't know," said Maude, "but I wouldn't be surprised if that sculptor fella, Jona Lewis, isn't one of 'em. You see him with Robertay pretty frequently."

"Ayuh, you got that right, Maude," Minerva said. "And didja ever notice that every one of his sculptures is a woman with big boobs? Bet Robertay just loves that!"

"Jesus, Minerva, you're as obsessed with Robertay's chest as the boys in this town are," Maude said.

"I think Simon Britton is probably on the board," said June, hoping to steer the conversation away from Robertay's anatomy.

"Right, him and that Toni…uh, Toni Ludlow," added Karen. "There might be one or two others, but I'd bet on those three, well, and Thomas. So that's four and Robertay makes five. Wonder if the police have talked with all them yet."

"I heard a buncha people said the painting was there when the reception was over," Maude said. "Guess that would make the key a pretty important discovery."

"Oh that Christly idiot Rendall Kalin thinks he's cracked the case

GEOFFREY SCOTT

wide open, for sure," Minerva said. "Ginnie Lynd over at the Tavern told me that he actually popped a button off his shirt he was so swole up. The jackass!"

"Well maybe that jackass really did crack the case," Caleb Rimes bellowed from the boys' table. Caleb's comment confirmed the ladies' suspicion that the men spent as much time listening in as they did talking amongst themselves.

Caleb was one of Rendall's few friends in town so it surprised no one at either table that he'd stick up for the constable. But his outburst upset the normal détente between the tables and soon the men were standing around the women and a cacophony arose. The men's conversation paralleled that of their peers, but that did little to soften the voices, conjectures, or swearing that now ensued.

John McTavish took it all in as he worked through his breakfast and several cups of coffee. Since the theft, he'd tried to keep busy with his artwork and his household projects, but he found himself loitering at various spots around town hoping that the topic of the theft would arise. Doing so, he'd learned much about the town folk; he hadn't learned nearly as much about the case.

Deciding that something sweet might aid his own reflection on the mystery, he ordered two of Trudy's molasses donuts with the intention of eating one and taking the other home for his mid-morning coffee break. Maggie had loved Trudy's molasses donuts while McTavish fancied himself a cinnamon sugar man. They'd agreed to disagree over which was the best until one morning they'd found only molasses donuts in the counter jar. As they sat down at a table, Maggie said, "You know, it wouldn't kill you to try one. Might even do you some good."

McTavish mumbled, made a face, and then bit into one of the slightly crusty confections. Expecting a sickly sweet glop of cake, McTavish was delighted by the rich texture and the intriguing taste. "What the hell," he said aloud before he realized it. A donut that he *knew* he didn't like couldn't possibly taste this good. Maggie had just smiled.

This morning, McTavish made more progress on his donut than on the mystery. The donut's exquisite flavor was part of the problem; his artist's eye was the other. As he ate his first donut, his attention focused on the second. In this case, however, it was the donut's shape that struck him rather than its potential as a snack. Among many things, artists deal with both positive and negative space. In one sense, a donut is defined by its positive space—the actual fried cake McTavish was thoughtfully chewing and the other one he was now studying. But equally important, composition-wise, was the empty interior. To his mind, that empty or negative space was just as critical to depicting a donut as the actual cakey ring. The size of the space, the regularity or irregularity of the space, and the configuration of the space would all contribute to an artist's rendering. Donut holes could be round or oval, smooth or craggy, thin or thick. As he rolled all of this over in his mind, McTavish realized the complexity of a donut's composition. Two other thoughts then pushed into his conscious mind. One was the ingenuity of Dunkin' Donuts in seeing a way to profit from a donut's negative space by selling donut "holes." The other was that, as integral as a donut's negative space was to an artist, to a donut eater, it mattered not a whit.

After finishing the first *Composition in Molasses* as McTavish dubbed his mental drawing, he took his time wrapping up the second. As he did so, it struck him that the Homer theft was much like the donut he held in his hand. In the empty center space was the crime itself; the crime only took shape as he and everyone else in town considered the people, events, timeline, places, and motives around it. Each of those things mattered individually, but it was in the interaction among them that the theft became real. The difference, of course, was that, until a donut is eaten, the negative space that helps define it remains constant. The negative space that is a crime, however, shifts and changes as the circumstances and evidence emerge. The crime donut that McTavish now saw in his mind had a very large hole with a very thin ring around it—for, he suspected, there were far more unknowns than knowns at this point.

McTavish wasn't sure that all this donut thinking was productive, but he left Lydia's with a full belly and a mind equally intrigued by drawing *and* crime-solving possibilities.

CHAPTER 9

So who owned the key that Rendall Kalin found? While the townsfolk speculated, Detective Chambers investigated. Grumpy that it was the department's most inept cop who'd made the discovery, Chambers was nevertheless excited about what seemed like the first real lead. Sure, they had the Park kid with the painting in his trunk, but Chambers worried about the missing pieces—How did the painting get there and when? Did Jimmy Park put it there or did someone else? How did no one see the crime? With Jimmy silenced by his lawyer, Chambers felt as if he was bouncing from one unanswered question to another. The key held out the possibility that some of the bouncing might stop.

Detective Chambers's first call was to Robertay Harding. He had to know how many keys were out there and who had them.

After four rings, however, Chambers heard, "I'm painting. Leave a message." Goddamn artists, he thought. Knowing that her beau, Thomas Beatty, couldn't fart without Robertay's say so, he drove over to Robertay's cottage in hopes of finding out if the old girl was working close by.

She wasn't, but Thomas was there. Detective Chambers tried to quiz him about the keys, but after Thomas couldn't even remember if he had one, he pushed the old artist as to where Robertay might be.

Thomas scratched his head with a paint-covered hand, smiled at the detective, and said, "Well, uh, I think she, well, I think she went… No that was yesterday…" Still smiling, Thomas walked over to the kitchen counter and picked up an index card with some writing on it. Handing it to Chambers, Thomas said, "She, Robertay that is, she wrote down where she was going because, well, because I sometimes forget…" Eventually, Chambers determined that Thomas had dropped Robertay at the far end of Cove Road to spend the day painting. He was to pick her up in an hour for lunch. Chambers volunteered to drive over and bring her back.

As he drove along Cove Road, Detective Chambers braced for the confrontation. On a good day, Robertay was New York prickly. He hadn't had many interactions with her, but he doubted that there were many good days. Chambers suspected Robertay was done with the theft and just wanted it to go away. She seemed to enjoy the initial notoriety. When questions about the safety and security of the Homer painting started to get more pointed, however, she had bristled. Chambers still felt the sting of Robertay's verbal lashes from the interview he'd conducted with her the morning after the crime was discovered.

"How in the hell am I supposed to know what happened," she had snapped as soon as the interview began. "You're the police. You know that Jimmy Park did not steal that painting. You'd have to be an idiot to think that! Why aren't you tracking down the real thief? Don't you have some fingerprints or DNA or CSI to tell you who did it?"

Chambers had held up his hand at that point and tried to take her methodically through the events of the previous evening. Robertay revealed nothing that had not been confirmed by at least a couple of other patrons, so he declared mercy on himself and ended the interview. He wasn't looking forward to a repeat performance with the Art Colony head.

Spotting her where Cove Road dead-ended, Chambers pulled over, closed his door as quietly as possible, and walked over to where Robertay worked. The seascape on her easel looked something like its subject, though clearly Robertay had taken artistic liberty with things like perspective and form. "Goddamn artists," he muttered again as he neared the work site.

Robertay jumped a bit when Chambers *ahemmed* his way into her consciousness. He braced for an attack and it came in full force. "Jesus H. Christ, constable, what in the hell do you think you're doing sneaking up on an artist in full bloom. Look what you made me do! It's going to take me an hour to correct that mess!" Chambers mumbled an apology, though he could see no damage to the painting that it hadn't already suffered.

"What the hell do you want?" Robertay asked. "Did you catch the thief? Is that why you're intruding on my space?"

"No, ma'am," Chambers said. "But we may have discovered an important clue and—"

"A clue?" Robertay shouted. "Who cares about a goddamn clue? Catch the person who committed the crime!"

"We're trying, Robertay, we're trying," said Chambers, trying to control his temper. "We can use your help." Normally the tactic of enlisting help from others softened them. Not so with Robertay.

"Well, isn't that just great! Now you're telling me that you can't do your job unless I help you?"

Biting his cheeks, his tongue, and anything else Chambers could think of, he soldiered on, "Ms. Harding, we found a key outside the back door to the gallery and we're wondering if you can help us figure out who it might belong to."

"Well, why in the hell didn't you say so?" Robertay asked. "That's simple enough. Thomas has one…no, that's not right. He had one, but I took it away because he kept losing it. So…well, all the board members have keys, so that's three… Oh, and then there's Larry Court. Larry looks after the building, so he's got a full set of keys." With that, Robertay turned back to her painting, apparently dismissing Chambers.

"That's' great, Ms. Harding, very helpful. I've already checked with Larry. He has his key and it works in the lock. So what I'd like to know

GEOFFREY SCOTT

is who the board members are and if it is possible that anyone else might have a key."

Irritated, Robertay continued painting, answering over her shoulder. "Don't even think that the Park boy has a key. He does not. The boy has talent, but he's a boy. One doesn't give a key to an important gallery to a boy, a fledgling."

Chambers wasn't sure how important the Colony gallery was, but he pushed on. "That's important information, Robertay. Who is on the board?"

Still refusing to look at the detective, Robertay said curtly, "Toni Ludlow, Jona Lewis, and Simon Britton are the current members of the board. Each of them would have a key."

"And none of them has reported losing one?" Chambers hoped for a bigger break.

"No, constable. These are responsible artists and members of the Colony board. They aren't the type to just lose a key. Now Larry… Larry is a different story. He's quite old, you know."

This comment inspired more cheek and tongue biting as Chambers suspected that Larry and Robertay were the same age. "I'll check with him…again," Chambers said.

Then remembering that he had told Thomas that he would bring Robertay home for lunch, Chambers made the offer. Anticipating another rebuke, he was surprised to see Robertay turn, smile, and say, "Why, officer, what a sweet offer. My friend Thomas is so forgetful. He would likely have left me all day." And with that, she quickly packed up her kit and reached out for Chambers to take her hand for the walk to his car.

I'm going to have a mouthful of cankers from this old broad, Chambers thought.

Chapter 10

As he drove back to town, Detective Chambers called Sergeant Levesque and asked him to contact all the Art Colony board members and have them meet him at the gallery with their keys to the back door. He also asked that Constable Artie Long go over immediately so that he could keep the artists corralled until Chambers got there.

Pulling into the gallery's front parking lot, Chambers saw Constables Long and Kalin talking with Toni Ludlow, a tall, raw, but attractive woman in her mid-forties. Ludlow's amused expression suggested that one of the two policemen had said something funny, inappropriate, or both. And since she was facing Kalin, he could only imagine the worst. Chambers greeted Ludlow, nodded to Long, and asked Kalin, "Constable, why aren't you out on patrol?"

"I heard you call in to the desk, sir, and, well, since I was the one who discovered the crucial piece of evidence, I figured you'd want me here," Kalin explained with a puppy-dog smile.

"We'll talk about it later, Kalin. Right now I want you back on patrol," Chambers said with anger suppressed. Kalin pouted, but turned on his heel and headed for his cruiser. Constable Long just rolled his eyes. Chambers said, "Okay, Artie, stay here and wait for the other board members while Ms. Ludlow and I check her key in the back door lock."

Artie nodded while Chambers and Ludlow walked toward the building.

Uncertain situations usually bring out people's nerves. And nerves mean that individuals brought into an investigation usually talk too fast and too much, and often need to be calmed down before any useful information can emerge. Not so with Toni Ludlow. She matched Chambers's stride and his quiet. Chambers let the silence continue, hoping that it might prod Ludlow to open up. He took note that it didn't. As they walked to the rear parking lot and the back door, Chambers asked simply, "Do you have your key?"

"I do," Ludlow replied and produced a long piece of coarse twine with a key at the end. Chambers took it from her and walked up the two steps to the back door. He fitted the key into the lock, twisted it, and turned the knob. Though the door squeaked, it opened with little effort. Chambers pulled the door closed and relocked it. He withdrew the key, handed it to Ludlow, and asked, "How long have you been on the Colony board?"

"About a year now."

Like pulling teeth, Chambers thought. "Is that how long everyone serves?"

"We all serve three-year terms."

Chambers thought Ludlow was finished speaking, but then saw her smile slightly as if to let on that she knew she had been dragging out the interview. "But our terms are staggered so that there is always a mix of new and old folks on the board. Robertay likes it that way."

"And what Robertay wants…" Chambers stopped and looked at Ludlow who smiled again and nodded. "Okay. Well thanks, Ms. Ludlow. I appreciate you taking the time to come over."

"Quite happy to, detective," Ludlow said. She then added, with what Chambers now thought of as a mysterious smile, "Nice to see you again."

Chambers escorted Ludlow to the front of the gallery. As he did so, he replayed in his mind the initial interview he had conducted with her the day after the theft was detected. Her cool, concise responses had struck him then, as had her intriguing, but ill-defined attractiveness. It took him a minute to recall her alibi—she and two artist friends had met for a nightcap at The Barlow House after the reception—but he remembered everything about what she wore…and that smile.

When Constable Long saw Detective Chambers walk Toni Ludlow to her car, he called over to Jona Lewis who had been waiting by his old pick-up. Lewis, a powerfully built man in his early 30s, seemed to be covered in a fine dust. As Chambers joined them, Lewis noticed the detective looking at his clothes. He said, "I'm a sculptor. The marble dust gets on ya and it just never seems to come off." The two shook hands and Lewis fished a single key from his pants pocket. Wiping away some dust he said, "I think you'll find it in fine order."

Chambers and Lewis walked around the building. Chambers walked up the stairs to the door, repeated the process he used for Ludlow's key, and found that it worked. As he relocked the door and withdrew the key, he asked Lewis if he had thought about anything new since they had last talked. "I've been going over it and over it, detective. I keep thinking there must have been something I missed. But nothing's come to me. As I told you at the station, I left before the thing ended. Had to pick up my dog from a neighbor before she went to bed. I just can't believe it's that Park boy. I don't know him all that well, but he just doesn't seem the sort to do something this stupid."

"And yet the painting was in his trunk. It can't be denied."

"True enough," said Lewis. "I guess you never know." As the two shook hands and walked toward the main parking lot, Chambers noted the difference in the two artists' demeanors. Might be something there, he thought.

Rounding the building, Chambers saw that Constable Long was alone. As Lewis got in his rusty truck and drove off, Chambers asked Long if the last artist had appeared. "Simpson? Silas? What's the guy's name?"

"Simon, sir, Simon Britton," Long replied. "He called and said he was coming along."

GEOFFREY SCOTT

At that moment, Long and Chambers saw an older, but well-maintained Cadillac pull into the gallery parking lot. A tall, elegant-looking man in his early 50s got out of the car and walked to the policemen. "So sorry I'm late," Britton said. "I had trouble finding my keys."

Chambers was about to tell him not to worry, when he saw the bunch of 20 or more keys in Britton's hand bound together in a tangle of key chains, wires, and rings. He marveled at the sight of the distinguished artist with a witch's brew of keys, two of which fell off in his hands as he looked through them. "Yes, I know, detective, they're quite a happy mess," Britton said with a forced smile. "But I have so many and I can't seem to organize them, so I just put them all together."

"Okay, let's try your key in the door. Which one is it?" Chambers asked.

"I'm honestly not sure," Britton admitted. "I don't think I've ever used it. But I'm sure it's there. I remember when Robertay gave it to me. I put it right on a ring so I wouldn't lose it." He beamed at this last remark as if he'd solved the secret of the Sphinx.

"Jesus," muttered Chambers as he walked toward the back door. Over his shoulder, he said, "You can stay there, Mr. Britton, while I check it out." Fumbling with the mass of keys, Chambers thought, "I oughta lock this guy up just for wasting my time." He then remembered that Ludlow's and Lewis's keys bore a Schlage logo. Searching through Britton's keys, Chambers found three with that brand, but none worked in the lock. In the interest of being thorough, and on the off chance that Robertay had given Britton a duplicate key on generic stock, Chambers tried all the rest of the keys to no avail. When he realized that the newly discovered key must be Britton's, Chambers smiled.

Walking around to the front of the gallery, Chambers asked Britton, "These are all of your keys, is that correct?" When Britton nodded, Chambers asked, "Have you had occasion to change out any of the keys over the last week or so?" Britton shook his head and the smile with which he'd greeted Chambers's return started to fade.

STEALING HOMER

"Is there a problem?"

"I'm afraid there is, Mr. Britton. None of your keys fit the back door lock." Chambers held up a hand as Britton started to protest. "I tried all of them." Taking Britton's right arm, Chambers steered him toward his car, saying, "Let's go down to the station and see if we can't sort all of this out."

Chapter 11

Simon was pacing when Jimmy Park arrived at his house that evening.

Simon had taken an early and active interest in Jimmy's artistic talent and had given the boy oil and watercolor lessons over the years. Simon's long-time partner, Ben Watkins, had died two years earlier. Nurturing Jimmy's interests had helped ease some of Simon's anxieties after Ben's death, and the boy had responded positively to the attention. Now, however, they were two men with different, but related problems.

Jimmy had heard about Simon's key fiasco, so he wasn't surprised to get a call asking him to come over. Bradley, who had been having supper with Jimmy and his parents, tagged along. Simon greeted Jimmy with a hug and a weak smile. "I seem to be in a most terrible fix."

"What happened," Jimmy asked as they all walked into Simon's shabby chic living room.

"Your key didn't work?" Bradley blurted out.

"Right to the point as always, eh, Bradley?" Simon replied. Jimmy noted the weariness in the older man's voice and the trace of annoyance at Bradley's rushing the story. Simon was a man to whom decorum, pace, and manners mattered. He was agitated, Jimmy knew, but Simon put up a brave front when confronted by folks like Bradley who were cut from stern Maine stock and just wanted the facts.

"Let Simon tell it his way, Bradley," Jimmy said softly. "I'll put some coffee on." As Jimmy left for the kitchen, he heard Bradley shift the conversation to the work he'd been doing in Simon's back yard.

"You're learning, Brad," Jimmy said to himself. He and Bradley, as unlike as any two Rascal Harbor boys, had formed an early and unshakeable bond. Bradley, the rugged star athlete, and Jimmy, the thin artist, yapped at each other about their respective failings—Bradley's impulsiveness and Jimmy's sensitivities. Neither, however, would tolerate criticism of his friend from others. As Bradley and Simon discussed the yard projects, Jimmy couldn't help but smile and think that, perhaps, his efforts to encourage Bradley to think a bit longer before he acted were paying off.

With coffee in hand and everyone settled into old, comfortable chairs, Jimmy encouraged Simon to tell his story.

"It was just awful, simply awful. I was so embarrassed! I got to the gallery late and in an absolute panic because I couldn't find my keys—"

"You're always losing your keys," Bradley said.

"Jesus, Bradley, shut up and let Simon talk!"

"Sorry, Simon," Bradley muttered.

Simon reached over and patted Jimmy's knee in gratitude and continued, "Well, as I said, I just couldn't find my keys and, when I did, well, you boys know that they're kind of a mess. I keep thinking that I should go through them and sort and organize them, but…well, anyway, I got to the gallery late and the policemen were standing there looking at me as if I were the last criminal on earth. I tried to explain, but that older one, Chambers, he just took my keys and left me standing there with the constable." Simon took a sip of coffee and a calming breath before resuming his story, "Well, the dear boy and I just stood there looking at each other with silly smiles on our faces. I tried to make a little small talk, but he just looked at me. He really wasn't mean or anything, he just—"

"He just stared at you, yeah, we get it…" Bradley said, but then quickly apologized. "Sorry, sorry, Simon."

Jimmy just smiled.

GEOFFREY SCOTT

After a theatrical pause, Simon began again, "It wasn't long though before the detective, I think that's his title, came storming back with an accusatory look on his face. 'It doesn't work!' he said. 'Your keys don't work!' He was practically foaming at the mouth!"

Jimmy realized at this point that Simon was getting warmed up and, as he did so, his story was ratcheting up on the drama scale. Listening in again, Jimmy heard Simon say, "I didn't know what to do, I mean, what could I do? I'd given the man my keys. I had no explanation for why none of them worked. I've never even used the key before... I, I, well, I tried to remain composed, but I fear all I did was look guilty."

At this point, Simon turned directly to Jimmy, put both hands on Jimmy's knees, and said, "James, you have to know that I would never steal that painting and that I would never, ever try to implicate you in a theft!" Simon's eyes brimmed with tears. "I would never do such a thing."

Jimmy reached over and pulled Simon's head toward his such that their foreheads touched. "I know you wouldn't, Simon, I really do." Releasing the older man's head, Jimmy said, "I don't know who or how or why or when, but I know you didn't set me up."

Beside them, Bradley roughly said, "I'd like to get my hands on the bastard...and it sure as hell better not be you, Simon!"

Simon looked stricken.

"Cut it out, Bradley," Jimmy said.

"Well, I'm just sayin'."

Simon dried his eyes. "Well, we won't be able to do that tonight, gentlemen, so let's talk about finer things. James, I so want to show you my latest drawings of my garden. I've been working in charcoal, something I've not done in years—the mess! But I'm having a most glorious time. Please come see."

As the two men rose, Bradley took his cue and said, "I'm outta here. I don't mind working in the gardens, but I don't have to get all arty over them. I'll walk home, Jimmy. See you tomorrow."

Simon grabbed Jimmy's arm and led him to the studio as Bradley left through the front door.

CHAPTER 12

After leaving Simon's, Jimmy drove over to McTavish's cottage. He knew that if he went home after visiting with Simon that his father would make some comment about "Hanging around with *that* guy" and his mother would ask, "What pretty cute little things did Simon bought lately? He's got so many of those talents for a bachelor!" Hoping to stay out until his parents went to bed, Jimmy knew that McTavish would be up and would be ready to talk about the theft, about art, and about Simon.

Before talking about those topics, Jimmy asked about the pile of crumpled paper overflowing the trash can beside McTavish's drawing table. Jimmy could see several sketches of hands tacked to the big bulletin board behind the table, but it appeared that there were far fewer on the board than on the floor. "Rough day?" Jimmy asked, nodding toward the trash can.

"Rough couple of days. You've got to create the image itself—the fingers, the nails on the fingers, the palm, or the back of the hand. And there's the space around all of those elements. A hand seems to be as much about the space around it as it is the hand itself."

Not sure what any of that meant, Jimmy said, "Maybe you ought to pull out the paints again. You might give yourself some purchase if you use a different medium."

"Maybe," McTavish muttered.

"Then again, you could go all Picasso-like and draw fingers and palms and wrists all over the place!"

McTavish rolled his eyes and nodded toward the kitchen rockers. "What's up with Simon and the key?"

Jimmy sat. "I guess it won't surprise you, but Simon made it sound like he got the third degree from the cops. Practically accused them of police brutality. Now I wouldn't put it past the chief…but the detective? Dad and Julian say he's a straight-up guy. So I suspect Simon is exaggerating."

"But what's the deal? Did his key fit or not?"

"Nope, and he's got no explanation for not having the key since he knows that Robertay gave him one. When none of his pile of keys fit the lock, they took him down to the station. He said he kept telling them the same thing—'I just don't understand it.'"

"Jesus, he's in a fix then, isn't he?" asked McTavish. "But then that's good news for you, no?"

"I don't know, John, I just don't know." Jimmy voice held a hint of discouragement. "I guess they made Simon go through the whole timeline again about what happened during and after the reception. The way he was babbling, though, I expect he made even less sense than when he was questioned the first time."

"Ah, that reminds me, we never got to that part of the story the other night. What did happen after the reception?"

"Julian made me swear not to say anything to the police, but I guess you can know." Jimmy paused. "It's going to take a cup of coffee though…or something a little stronger?"

"You have yet to reach the magical age of 21, James Park, and the last thing you need right now is to get picked up with a DUI. Your father would skin you, and then he'd skin me, and he'd be right to do both of us. But I will let you have a little of my secret blend!"

"Okay, fine." Jimmy knew that McTavish's secret blend was really just a mix of Eight O' Clock and Café du Monde coffees.

STEALING HOMER

Once McTavish had the coffee brewing, he sat beside Jimmy in his rocker and the boy recounted the events that followed the Homer reception.

"So last time we talked about what happened at the reception up to the time you left," Jimmy started. "After Robertay got order restored, the thing began to wind down. The little hugs and air kisses and good wishes got going and people, especially the Portland people, started drifting away." Jimmy had every artistic sensibility, but he also had a Mainer's intolerance for faked emotions. Egged on, he could do a hilarious caricature of the art crowd's greetings and goodbyes. "So once the locals drained the last of the wine, it was Thomas, Simon, and me left to clean up. Robertay fluttered around for a while, but said she was too overcome from the evening to help. We weren't really sure what to do with the Homer, so we just pulled the unveiling cloth back over it, swept the floors, took out the garbage, and locked up."

"Who locked up?" McTavish asked, sensing a lead.

"Well, nobody actually locked up. I just pushed the button on the inside of the door, closed it, and it locked itself."

"So no one had to use a key to lock the door," McTavish said, disappointed.

"No. I thought about that. False trail though. But that's why the key that the police found has got to mean something. Someone had to use it to get back into the building and steal the painting. 'Cause, unless it's a grand conspiracy among Simon, Thomas, and me, then.... Jesus, John, do you think the police think it could be the three of us?"

"Hard to say. Until the mess around Simon's key, you were the only real suspect. Finding that key complicates things."

"I suppose it does, though I honestly can't see Simon stealing the painting."

"Did he know about your trunk latch and does he need the money?" McTavish asked.

"Well, everyone knows about my trunk. Dad didn't exactly do an artistic design when he wired it closed. Turns out a trunk latch for a

1983 Ford Fairmont is a hard item to find. I know it doesn't look like much, but I keep it running like a top."

"One of your many talents, James. So what about Simon's finances?"

"That's a little less clear. I think most of the money he and Ben had was actually Ben's. And when Ben died, I think most of that went to his sister's kids. I don't think Simon got much at all. He's never said, but that's the impression I have. Oh, and Bradley is always complaining that Simon is late in paying him for the work he does."

"Simon seems to live a pretty lavish life at least by Rascal Harbor standards."

"Agreed," Jimmy said. "I wonder if the police have put all that together."

"Wouldn't surprise me. And I wouldn't want to be in that detective's sights."

"I think the chief is worse. Dad says he's gunning for me. Dad also heard the chief was upset when the key was found because it screwed up the possibility that I was the only suspect."

"Yes, but I suspect Chief Miles has no special tolerance for Simon, either."

"Oh, god! I wonder if they think it was Simon and me together! I was joking before about a conspiracy, but what if the police really think there is one and it's Simon and me?" The boy looked genuinely distressed at this possibility.

"Maybe, but what about Thomas? You said he was there at the closing."

"Right, right, Thomas was there. He and Simon both offered me a lift to the garage—"

"A lift to the garage? Why would you need a lift to the garage?"

"Oh, right, you didn't know. I had a flat tire that night. Must have caught a nail or something on the way to the gallery and it went flat. I didn't have a spare, so Thomas and Simon both said they'd give me a ride to the garage to get one. I went with Thomas because Simon said that he'd give me a ride, but I'd have to be quick because he wasn't feeling all that well. He said it was probably the cheap wine. So I went with Thomas to get a spare and a jack. But while we were at the garage, Thomas got a call from Robertay. She demanded to know where he was and that he get home immediately. He tried to explain, but you know Robertay. I knew it was going to take me a while to find a tire and a jack so I told him it was okay if he left and that I'd get Bradley to give me a ride. Thomas looked relieved and took off."

Taking all this in, McTavish asked, "Okay, then what happened?"

"Not much to tell. Bradley came right over. We fixed the flat, then Bradley drove home, and I drove to Portland. You know what happened after that."

"I do and I don't. Somehow that painting got out of the gallery and into your trunk and, I hate to admit it, but it seems like Simon had the most direct access. Do the police know all of this?"

"Probably, though they don't know it from me. Julian won't let me say a word. But I'm guessing they know all or most of it from Thomas and Simon. Oh, and from Bradley. He talked to the detective, too."

"If the gossip at Lydia's is to be believed, then Thomas didn't have a key so he couldn't have gotten back in to steal the painting. And you didn't have a key. So that leaves only Simon. And it was Simon's key that the police found."

"Jesus," Jimmy murmured. "Poor Simon."

"Maybe 'poor Simon,' but maybe 'asshole Simon' if he's the one who stole the Homer. Maybe he didn't mean to set you up, maybe he thought he'd be able to get the painting out of your trunk in a day or two later. Regardless, it's looking more and more likely that Simon's the thief."

"Or Simon and me," Jimmy sighed.

"Or Simon and you."

Chapter 13

It was Simon *and* Jimmy who Detective Chambers thought about as he drove to the station that morning. "And" rather than "or" sounded intriguing to him.

As he turned into the department parking lot, Chambers saw Jumper Wilson walking toward the town hall. Though the October days were gaining a chill, Jumper still wore only a T-shirt with his worn khakis and Converse. No one knew for sure where Jumper came from, how he got to Rascal Harbor, or even what his real name was. Jumper just appeared one day and became a town fixture. Chambers assumed that the man might have introduced himself as Jump*er* at one point, but Mainers love to substitute an "ah" for any "r," so everyone called him Jump*ah* Wilson.

Despite his name, Jumper was a walker who roamed the Harbor streets with no apparent purpose other than to talk with whomever would engage him. That wasn't as hard as one might think for Jumper's T-shirts always inspired comment. Handwritten, they looked a bit like ransom demands as the letters featured different sizes, letter types, and colors. Invariably, however, they offered a different take on a familiar saying, world event, or whatever seemed to be on Jumper's mind. *Fish or cut bait*, one said, *but don't cut bait in a donut shop*. Another simply asked, *Are you friend or fowl?* Chambers's favorite to date was *Don't ask, don't tell…don't smoke, don't fidget, don't fart, don't fu…* with the last part being tucked into Jumper's khakis. These shirts, worn alone in spring, summer, and fall, and under an old parka in the winter, inspired all manner of reaction. In a town with more than its share of eccentrics, however, Jumper had lots of company on the weird end of the scale.

Jumper's T-shirt caught Chambers off guard today, however. It read, *Winslow's homer scored two.* Unsure whether to take it as a sign of his insight into the crime or just a cosmic joke, Chambers decided to interpret it as the first.

❦

At the same time, all thoughts were on Simon at Lydia's back tables. Caleb Rimes had learned of Simon's misadventure at the gallery on the previous day. He wouldn't say how he knew, but folks at both tables assumed it was one more news drop from Caleb's buddy Constable Kalin. Standing at the entry to the hallway that separated the two back tables, Caleb fielded questions, jabs, and suppositions from both sides:

"For Christ's sake, Caleb, you'd believe that idiot Rendall if he said he was Jesus H. Christ!"

"Do you really think Simon B. could be involved?"

"Course he is, it's his key they found."

"How many more folks are likely to get snared up in this mess?"

"So is Jimmy Park in the clear now?"

"Caleb, Jesus, when was the last time you changed that shirt of yours?"

"Why in the world would Simon steal that paintin'? They say he's got more money than God!"

"They also say that God ain't as rich as he was before the damn Democrats took over."

"I bet Chief Miles is smiling now that he can harass another one of the gays."

"What was that last thing you said, Ray?"

GEOFFREY SCOTT

"I always wondered about Simon…"

"Hell, you wondered about Ronald Reagan!"

"Remember when that buck-toothed Jimmy Carter came to town one summer. Jesus, didn't that guy talk some funny!"

And so it went. The conversation ping-ponged between tables, with Caleb clarifying and confusing matters by turns, sweating and swearing when the comments turned back to him, and gesticulating enough to get in Julia Nisbett's way as she brought food and dishes into and out of the kitchen. "Get your fat ass out of my hallway, Caleb Rimes," Julia demanded on the third pass. "This ain't Meet the Press nor CSI neither. Go solve the crime of the century somewhere else." Caleb grumbled, pulled up his pants, and stomped out.

❁

More talk filled the air at Gary's Garage where old friends and new stopped by to congratulate Gary on the news that Jimmy seemed to be off the hook. Gary's protests that Jimmy was hardly in the clear went largely unheard as the hearty cheers, thumps on the back, and victory signs continued. McTavish stood in a corner and watched, knowing Gary's anguish. The two had talked about the very good possibility that Simon and Jimmy might be yoked together as twin suspects. That possibility only grew as Gary and McTavish contemplated the pressure Chief Miles was likely to exert for a quick resolution and one that put two members of the local gay community behind bars. "Goddamit, Professker, Jimmy just can't catch a break on this thing," Gary said.

McTavish agreed. "I know Jimmy didn't do it, and I can't really believe that Simon did. But Miles, being Miles, is going have them in his sights."

❁

STEALING HOMER

Over at the *Gazette*, Nellie Hildreth and her staff held off mocking up the week's paper as the news about Simon broke around them. "Do you think he'll be arrested? And how long can we wait to find out?" Rich Reed, the managing editor, asked.

"Hell if I know," Nellie said. "The police don't always run on the same schedule as the paper." Turning to Sarah McAdams, the paper's only real reporter, Nellie continued, "Sarah, let's give you until four to see what you can dig up and then we'll run with what you've got." As Sarah nodded, Nellie turned back to Rich and asked, "Meantime, did you get Dorothy's obit placed?"

"I did, but holey moley, Nellie, you kinda pushed the limits on that one."

"I did not," Nellie yelled. "Hell, I just said what everyone knows about that old girl."

Rich read the text aloud, "Dorothy Pointer, aged 90 something, died of terminal crankiness leaving not a soul to care. Pointer, *nee* Williams, came from a prominent Massachusetts family, or so she told anyone who would listen. She summered each year at the family cottage on Sunset Point. Her husband, Winchester, died 10 years ago, likely to avoid Dorothy's accumulating wrath; her two girls, Maxine and Lisbeth, stopped visiting the next year. Kind folks said Dorothy could be a "pill;" less kind ones said something a little stronger…"

Here, Rich stopped reading, turned to Nellie, and said, "Why did you pull your punch at the end? You practically called her every kind of bitch up to that point, but then you backed off."

"I wondered if you'd notice that," Nellie said with a smirk. "I actually liked the old bird, so I decided to temper the truth a little."

"Damn, if that's tempering the truth for someone you like, I can't imagine what you'd say about someone you didn't."

"Stick around, boy, you'll find out soon enough."

CHAPTER 14

McTavish swore as he drove down to his cottage and saw his brother and sisters and a bunch of kids piling out of cars and trucks. "Ah shit, forgot all about them coming over today." He waved and forced a smile. It was McTavish's turn to host a family gathering. Because he'd forgotten they were coming, he hadn't laid in any food. He now tried to think where he could take them all for lunch that wouldn't end up bankrupting him. Mark, Ruth, and their broods ate a lot; he feared for his bank balance.

Soon after their brother moved to Rascal Harbor, Mark and Ruth had insisted that the Maine-based siblings make a pact to see each other more often. McTavish suspected a good part of their reasoning, and the only reason Giselle ever agreed, reflected their concern about him following Maggie's death. They never said so, of course, or at least never said so in front of him, but he appreciated the gesture even if he didn't always look forward to the visits.

Today it was his turn to host, and he'd forgotten all about it. The McTavish cupboard was never bare—he really could take care of himself. But with all the McTavishes in his doorway, he knew that his larder would not be up to the task.

He needn't have worried. Mark and Ruth knew their college professor older brother to be absent minded and so had taken matters into their own hands. They'd brought food enough for several families and were now transporting it into McTavish's unlocked cottage. "John, you really ought to lock your door," Ruth said over her shoulder. "You just can't be too careful these days."

Especially around my own family, McTavish thought. But he put on a smile, braced for the ribbing he would take for being unprepared, and hoped that Giselle and Martin would stay on after Mark and Ruth bundled their families back home.

Giselle and Martin, long-time vegans, always packed their own food. Neither enjoyed watching the meat fest that was a standard McTavish meal, but neither did they make a fuss. Both had grown up in families that ate whatever they had—and meat and eggs and cheese and potatoes were what they typically had. Giselle and Martin had chosen a different culinary path as adults, but they did not lord their clean, violence-free eating preferences over their families. Of course, that did not stop Mark and Ruth from chiding them about being "gatherers and grazers," but the sting had largely worn off.

"John, I see you laid in some yogurt and pickles and a package of hot dogs," Mark's voice boomed as he filled McTavish's refrigerator. "Must have thought you were going to feed an entire army today! Oh, and look, you've got mustard, too! We could have a real feast!"

"Lay off, Mark," said Giselle. "No refrigerator on the planet could hold enough food to fill that belly of yours."

"Ha! Good one, Miss Granola." Mark patted his stomach. "I earned every ounce of this gut and I'm planning to add another couple more today."

"Not too many more ounces, I hope," said Ruth.

Mark's wife, Amy, added, "You grow that belly much more and you won't be able to see your feet." Mark grinned, most everyone else laughed, and the day got started.

As Amy, Ruth, and Ruth's husband Ronald, put out the food, Mark, Giselle, and Martin appraised McTavish's art and cottage work. The three had little to say about the first. Studying the drawings of the hands that were pinned over McTavish's table, Giselle and Martin pronounced them "life-like." Mark also seemed interested, lingering over them longer than McTavish might have guessed.

"Yup, they do look pretty life-like, but Christ, John, if you spend that much time and effort drawin' a couple of hands, how long's it going to take you to do a whole body? You ain't got that many years left, old boy!"

The family was far more complimentary of McTavish's work in installing trim work and doors on one of the two closets in the cottage. McTavish was no fine craftsman, but he took his time, he measured twice in order to cut only once, and he used chisels, planes, and sandpaper to make corners tight. The whitewash stain he used throughout met with most everyone's approval for it would neither nick nor scape as a painted surface might.

"Pretty fine work, for a professor," Martin said.

"Fine enough for a professor *or* for a plumber," Giselle teased lightly. And so the artwork and the cottage work passed enough muster such that the group moved on to lunch-time conversations that centered on topics other than McTavish.

Except that they did insofar as he was a resident of Rascal Harbor and the Rascal Harbor art theft was a topic Mark, Ruth, and their families had come ready to discuss. Mark, Amy, Ruth, and Ronald peppered McTavish with questions. Giselle and Martin sat back and enjoyed the inquisition. "You're doing well," Giselle whispered to her brother at one point, "for a guy who doesn't know shit."

McTavish smiled.

On everyone's mind were questions about who the key suspects were and which one was the most likely culprit. McTavish wasn't sure if the theft would be all that newsworthy in the days before the Internet, but it was now. And it was clear that Mark, Ruth, and their spouses were staying on top of the breaking scene.

After McTavish's third protest that he didn't really know much of what was going on, Mark said, "Well Jesus, John, you do know all these characters, don't you? Surely you've got an opinion of who did what."

"Well, yes, but an opinion is all it is, and I can't say that I know any more than what you've heard."

"It is exciting though," said Ruth. "And here you are right in the middle of the mystery. So lay it out for us."

And so he did. McTavish mustered up his professorial self and delivered a monologue worthy of his best classes. He described the discovery of the painting and the reason it caused such a stir among the art intelligentsia. He began to lose his crowd when his discourse on Winslow Homer's style and importance ran long, so he shifted over to a slightly exaggerated recounting of the reception and the various art types on the scene. Mark and Ruth snorted as McTavish portrayed the Portland dealers and artists and their garish outfits and gestures. McTavish drew some laughter—even from the attendant children—as he recalled the fracas when the Homer painting hit the floor. More solemn, thoughtful looks surfaced as he laid out the incidents that followed the reception.

No one interrupted his account, a fact that McTavish put down partly to his embroidered story line and partly to the fact that they'd all been taught not to talk with their mouths full of food. He finished about the time that everyone's hunger slaked. At that moment, the questioning began again, coming from all sides and in all forms:

"So who did it, Uncle John?"

"Jesus, do you think the robber might be still at large?"

"How do you feel safe when you don't lock your door?"

"Isn't it possible that the whole thing is just a misunderstanding?"

"Are you sure you told us everything?"

"When is low tide today? I want to go down to the beach!"

"I've given it some thought and it seems that this Simon whatever his name is has to be the thief."

"I would have agreed, but now I'm wondering if it really wasn't the Park kid."

"I bet it's that police chief."

"What happens to the painting now?"

"Can you paint as good as Winston Homer?"

"You've just got to wonder what's happening to this country when a painting in small-town Maine gets stolen."

Ruth made this last point as Ronald, Mark, and Amy shook their heads in agreement. The steam left the conversation and the kids left the table. Mainers, at least the McTavish Mainers, aren't much for lollygagging once a meal and its attendant conversation were over. The group broke up to clear the table, remark about how good the food was, remind McTavish that they'd have starved were it not for Mark and Ruth's ministrations, and belch.

The last was Mark's forte as was his response as Amy shushed him. "Well, you know, in some cultures a big burp is a sign of respect for the meal taken," Mark said.

"And in some cultures," Giselle said, "they drink piss."

This comment sent Martin and the kids into hysterics, and Ruth and Ronald into red-faced embarrassment. "Jesus, you got me on that one, little sister," Mark bellowed. "Though let's see…is piss vegan?"

"Only to a pisspot brother," Giselle replied dryly.

Giselle's comment coincided with screams from outside the cottage. The kids had been plinking one another with fallen acorns. The last few had found tender spots and so a great howling had begun. Mark and Ruth interpreted all of this as a sign to pack up their respective families and caravan home. McTavish felt that their words of "Good to see everyone" and "We'll have to do this again soon" expressed genuine sentiments and he was a little surprised that his responses were equally so. He really couldn't imagine the family ever spending more than a couple of hours peacefully together. Given the many ways families can tear themselves apart, however, he decided he would take what he had and smile.

His smile broadened as he and Giselle walked back into the cottage. Martin was tending the wood stove as they entered and he handed them both oversized pours of a modest Cabernet.

"Well, you did it, big brother," Giselle said as she settled into one of the kitchen rockers. "Or, you mostly did it. You did provide the location…and the mustard! You've set a new standard for hosting the clan."

"I did indeed. And nary a drop of blood was shed. Might be a low standard, but it's still a standard."

"Would have been easier if Maggie were here," Giselle said gently.

McTavish let the comment settle for a minute before he responded. "Aye. She'd have remembered the food and drink…and the napkins and placemats. And she'd have put the kibosh to the acorn wars before the crying started."

"She was a good old gal, brother John. You doing okay?"

Again, McTavish hesitated before responding. "Mostly." He took a long drink of wine. "Some days are harder than others. I try to keep busy, keep my mind and body moving. But I can always hear her voice."

"Too bad you didn't hear her voice say, 'Pick up some grub for your family's visit!'" Martin said and laughed. Giselle shushed him, but snickered as she did so.

"I expect I'll hear a good deal from her tonight about that one," McTavish admitted.

At that, the three sat back in their chairs and let the heat from the stove and the quiet at the end of the day wash over them. McTavish knew he ought to have more to say, but Maggie had always carried their social interactions. He was now consciously trying to offer a bit more of himself whenever he engaged in a conversation. He suspected, however, that Maggie would downgrade the B+ rating he gave himself to something more like a C. A middling social grade was fine with Giselle and Martin, though, as neither were big talkers, nor would either of them push McTavish to open up emotionally. They knew his grief and they respected his right to hold onto it as tightly as he wanted. It's not true that Mainers are unfeeling, but it is true that few wear their feelings clearly on their sleeves. McTavish sometimes wished he could just say what he felt. For now, however, he'd take the clear and considered comfort that Giselle and Martin offered in their warm and graceful silence.

Chapter 15

Giselle and Martin left before their wine consumption would have gotten them arrested. McTavish wished he saw them more often. Though they were nearly as quiet as he, McTavish felt that his social skills might significantly improve if Giselle and Martin lived closer. "Okay, Mags," he said to himself and to Maggie. "I wish I'd paid more attention to your instruction. This social stuff seems over my head at times."

McTavish smiled at this thought because he knew how Maggie would respond, "Jesus, John, you talk all day! You talk with students, you talk with your colleagues, you even talk with an administrator or two. Why is it so hard to talk with regular people?"

When he didn't throw up his hands and shrug, McTavish would try to explain the difference between everyday talk and talk about history and college courses and committee work. "Not all of my school stuff is interesting, but it's talk about *something*," he would say. "That social stuff about who's talking to whom and for how long before they have another fight, the stuff about families and marriages breaking up…it's just—"

"It's just *life*," Maggie would interrupt. "John, it's about life, the lives people lead. I would think that, as a historian, you'd see that and understand that it's endlessly fascinating."

"Maybe so, Mags, maybe so," McTavish would admit, though he did so more in hopes of ending the conversation than because he was convinced.

Most cancers leave a long trail. Drugs and a hearty constitution had spared Maggie a good part of the associated pain, and a life well lived had spared her any regrets. And though her death should have been no surprise, McTavish felt blindsided.

McTavish's standard approach to life's problems was deal with them only when he had to, and only then if Maggie refused to or couldn't. Maggie had talked openly about her illness and its inevitable outcome and McTavish had listened closely and responded in kind. But his mind would reach no conclusions. It was as if his brain could think only halfway into whatever point Maggie was making, and then hop over to something else, and then hop again. The experience left him *thinking* that he was prepared to deal with their son, their house, their insurances, their lives…and yet it didn't.

Maggie had well prepped her wide circle of friends. They managed her funeral and McTavish and most of the aftermath of retracting a friend's life once lived. And although they disagreed with his decision, they even managed his transition to Rascal Harbor and they encouraged his rejuvenation through art. They were as fine a group of friends as any person might have. But they were Maggie's friends and, though McTavish accepted their assistance with grace, he could gain no purchase as their friend. In moving to Rascal Harbor, he left his job and his home and his acquaintances, but mostly he left the life that Maggie had created for them. McTavish had started…and stopped many letters of appreciation to the women who had seen him through. He knew that it mattered to them to hear that he was settling in and that they could not feel their obligation to Maggie was met until he was. Yet the words came slowly and awkwardly and, in the end, the letters ended up in the same trash can that so many of his hand drawings did. He would write to them eventually because Maggie would remind him to do so. Just not now.

Drifting down this road usually meant that McTavish headed for the Bushmills bottle. And he might have done so that night but for the arrival of Jimmy Park and Bradley Little. Since they knocked loudly and entered brimming with excitement, McTavish presumed they had something to share related to the case.

"What's up, boys?" McTavish asked quietly. "This really isn't the best time."

"It won't take long, John, but this is important and we wanted your advice," Jimmy said smiling broadly.

Inviting them to sit, McTavish sighed. "Okay, let's have it."

Jimmy started, "So Bradley and I were going over the theft again. This must be like the fiftieth time, right Brad?" Bradley nodded his head, excitement on his face. Jimmy said, "You know, the whole scene, top to bottom, just looking for anything that didn't seem right."

McTavish nodded. "Like most of the town has."

"Right, right," Jimmy said, "but we think we've got something now. Well, Bradley thinks he might have something. And I've got something else."

Turning to Bradley, McTavish asked, "So what did you come up with?"

Seemingly a little embarrassed that all eyes were on him, Bradley started in halting fashion. "Well, it really might be nothing, but—"

"Just tell it!" Jimmy said.

"Okay, okay, I'm going to, just give me a minute." Taking in a long breath, Bradley continued. "So I just kept thinking about that whole night and my mind kept coming back to the beginning, when I was stamping the people's hands. I couldn't figure out why my brain would do that, but then I remembered something." At this comment, his smile broadened and then flickered, "But it's a long shot."

"It's getting late, Bradley," McTavish said, though he tried to hide his growing exasperation.

"It was the ink," Bradley blurted out, "the ink pad!"

"The ink pad?"

"Yup, the ink pad." Bradley's confidence grew. "I remembered that I fumbled the ink pad when Simon Britton was coming through. It fell on the floor, and when Simon picked it up, he had ink all over his fingers. He tried to wipe it off with his handkerchief but, that ink—well, it sticks on."

"Okay…what's that got to do with…?" McTavish shrugged.

"Don't you see?" Jimmy said. "It's entirely possible that Simon left a print on the painting with that red ink!"

"Possible? Hardly," McTavish replied. "If the police had a fingerprint, especially if it was one of Simon's, he'd be sitting in jail."

"Well, right, of course…but maybe there's something about the ink that *would* tie Simon to the crime. If it's not me, it's got to be Simon."

"It's gotta be Simon," Bradley said. "I mean, who else could it be? It was his key at the back door—"

"And, he had the opportunity!" Jimmy said. "That's my contribution." Catching a quick breath, he continued, "Remember I told you about what happened after the reception, how I had a flat tire and had to get a ride to the garage? And remember who took me and why?"

"Wasn't it Simon? No…wait, it wasn't Simon, though I don't remember why. It was Thomas who gave you the ride," McTavish said.

"Exactly," Jimmy said, triumphantly. "It was Thomas who drove me over and then got called home by Robertay."

"Ah, now I see where you're going. You think that gave Simon an opportunity to steal the painting."

"Right," Jimmy and Bradley said at the same time.

"And his keys are always in a mess," said Bradley. "So he coulda easily dropped the back door key once he unlocked the door."

"I've got to think the police have considered all these possibilities." McTavish's interest in the boys' stories now piqued. "Do they know the story of the ink pad and the flat tire?"

Geoffrey Scott

"Well, who knows?" Jimmy said. "I haven't told them because Julian told me not to. And Thomas...can you imagine what kind of gobbled up story he told? So that leaves Simon. And if he told them what happened, he could have spun it a hundred different ways!"

"I suppose...and what about the ink pad?" McTavish asked.

"I just remembered it," Bradley said. "I didn't think of it when the police were talking to me the next day."

"It's all starting to click," Jimmy said. "Think about it. Simon's got the opportunity—that story about the cheap wine—well, Bradley takes out his trash so he's seen the wine that Simon buys and the prices show that he's not buying the best." Bradley nodded at this report. "So maybe Simon really is hurting financially and saw the Homer as a way to make some money. Simon's been around a long time and he knows a lot of art dealers and I'd bet they're not all on the up and up."

"But why would he put it in your trunk?" asked McTavish. "That doesn't make any sense."

"Maybe he got spooked?" Bradley said.

Jimmy snapped his fingers. "Or, more likely, he needed a place to keep it safe until the heat died down over it being stolen. I mean who would look in my trunk? Maybe he figured it would take a while for the theft to be discovered and he could get the painting out whenever he wanted."

"Hmmm, these pieces aren't much on their own, but when you put them together..." McTavish said.

"That's what we're thinking," Jimmy said. "So we wanted to get your thoughts on it all and on what we ought to do."

"Well, you've got my thoughts on your hunches; they do seem to add up. What do you mean about what you ought to do?"

"Should we go to the police?" Bradley asked. "Go and tell them the whole thing? How we've cracked the case for them?"

"I'm not sure I'd go quite that far," McTavish said. Turning to Jimmy, he said, "You've got pieces, but that's really all they are at this point. And Julian isn't likely to change his mind about you going to the police now."

STEALING HOMER

"Right, right," said Jimmy. "So we were thinking that Bradley ought to go. If he tells them about the ink and my side of the story after the reception, then maybe that will get the police firmly on the right track."

"It's possible."

"Damn right, it's possible, that goddamned Simon," Bradley muttered.

"I still can't believe it fully," Jimmy said. "But if I think that Simon didn't actually intend to set me up, then it feels a little better." After a moment, Jimmy asked McTavish, "So do you think Bradley ought to go to the police and lay it all out?"

"I suppose...I suppose."

"That's what we think, too," Jimmy said. "Just think, this thing might be over soon!"

"I suppose," McTavish repeated.

Chapter 16

After dropping Bradley at his house, Jimmy drove home excited to relate the emerging ideas and plan of action. "Maybe, just maybe, this thing will be over," he said to himself.

In the kitchen, Jimmy found his father and mother sitting at the kitchen table talking quietly. He suspected the topic was financial as Gary and Ruby rarely talked quietly. He wanted to blurt out his news, but didn't want to interrupt. He needn't have worried.

"Dimmy, come sit wit us. We hardly don't see you no more these days," Ruby called out.

As he sat, Jimmy said, "I know, Mom. It's just I've been trying to keep busy so my brain doesn't explode. And there's plenty to do with school and my art work and weekends at the garage."

"We know, we know, Dimmy. It's what me and your dad was just talkin' about. We worried about you, Dimmy," Ruby said. At this note, Gary raised his head and looked at his son for the first time since he'd entered the room. Jimmy couldn't read those eyes.

"You doin' okay, Dimmy? We worried about you," Ruby repeated. "You been looking like something the cat dragged in the outhouse." Jimmy smiled. His mother could turn any phrase on its head.

"Well, I think I've got some good news, Mom," Jimmy said. "There might be a break in the case."

Both sets of parental eyes sharpened at this report, and Ruby called out to Jimmy's older sister Louise to come join them. Louise, who favored her father's lanky build and dour attitude, reluctantly turned off the TV and strolled into the kitchen.

"Ah, the great art thief returns," Louise said, but then rubbed Jimmy's hair to show that she meant no offense. "Come to rip off the family Rembrandts?"

"Knock it off, Louise," Gary said. Jimmy noticed two empty cans of Budweiser on the counter and a third in his father's hand.

"No, Louise, but I think some things are about to happen," Jimmy said.

Now the center of the Park family's attention, Jimmy told the story of his and Bradley's thinking and of their visit with McTavish.

Gary, Ruby, and Louise listened keenly to Jimmy's account. From time to time Ruby prompted, "Yes, yes, what else?" and Gary muttered. "That goddamn Simon. I wish you'd never got mixed up with him."

Louise kept her peace throughout, nodding at some points, looking skeptical at others. Once Jimmy finished, she said, "I don't know, Jimmy, seems pretty speculative."

"Speck…what?" asked Ruby. "You mean specific? Yup, I think it's pretty specific." Jimmy smiled; Louise looked at the ceiling.

Gary shook his head. "No, Ruby, she means it's just talk, it's all up in the air."

"What's up there?" Ruby asked. "The boys they got it all figured out!"

"Ma, all they've got figured out are some possibilities," said Louise. "They don't have any evidence."

"But Bradley, he tell 'em, he tell them polices and then Dimmy be scotch free," Ruby said. "That Bradley, he do anything for Dimmy."

"All he needs to do is tell the police what happened," Jimmy said. "And then we have to hope that there's some evidence of the ink."

"That's a lot of hoping," Gary said.

CHAPTER 17

Encouraged by Jimmy and McTavish, and eager to enter the fray, Bradley showed up at the police station early the next morning. Upon entering the lobby half an hour later, Detective Chambers saw an anxious Bradley Little jump up and rush over to him.

"I really gotta talk with you, sir. I think I've got somethin' you'll want to know."

"Okay, hang on, son," Chambers replied. "Let's go into my office and you can tell me your story." Chambers knew that Little chummed around with the Park boy so his suspicion radar began blinking. "Can I get you something to drink?"

"No, sir," Bradley said, calming a bit. "I'm just hoping to clear Jimmy." Chambers's radar increased its measure.

Settling into office chairs, Chambers asked, "So what have you got, Bradley?"

Sitting forward, Bradley began. "Well, I've been thinking about this crime a lot. I was there that night and Jimmy is my friend and I work for Simon and, well, I can't shake it out of my head. But there just seemed like something I couldn't put my finger on, and then it come to me." At this admission, Bradley snapped his fingers. "The ink pad!"

"The ink pad?" Chambers repeated, clearly confused. "What ink pad?"

"The ink pad that I was using to stamp the hands at the reception! I mean I think I told you that that was my job when you talked to me the next day, right? What didn't come to me until last night was when it fell."

"What do you mean 'when it fell'?"

Prompted, Bradley told the story of how he'd fumbled the ink pad and stamp when Simon Britton came through the door and that Simon had tried to catch it. In failing to do so, however, Simon had gotten ink on his fingers only some of which came off when he wiped them with a handkerchief.

"Okay..." said Chambers, failing to see the importance of this news. "Well, dontcha see it, sir? The ink I mean. If there was any ink on the painting, like a fingerprint or something..."

"There were all kinds of fingerprints on the painting, but then lots of people touched the painting when it was knocked over."

Bradley's face fell a bit at this news. "Oh, I guess that makes sense." Looking down at his feet as if to collect his thoughts, Bradley brightened up again. "But that's not all I came to tell you!"

"Oh?"

"Nope." Bradley smiled slyly. "I've been putting some things together."

"Such as?" Chambers sensed he was wasting time with this boy.

Winding up, Bradley said, "Well, I've been thinking about who had a motive to steal that painting. Jimmy's poor, but he's not stupid. What would he do with the painting once he had it? Jimmy's just a kid. He wouldn't know where to fence it."

Chambers smiled at the boy's junior detective language. Too much TV, he thought.

Bradley steamed on. "And then, of course, Simon's key to the back door gets found, but everyone's like, 'Simon's rich!' and 'Simon's got all kinds of money!' like that would mean that he'd never consider stealing a valuable painting." Catching his breath, Bradley continued. "Well, I happen to know that Simon's not as rich as he lets on. I work for him so I oughta know. Sometimes it's two-three weeks before he pays me and more than once he's had to delay it even longer 'until my invest-

GEOFFREY SCOTT

ment check comes in' he says." Bradley made air quotes and pitched his voice to echo Simon's.

"Well, I was talking to Jimmy, and he reminded me about Simon not giving him a ride home after he found out he had a flat tire. That Simon said he was sick from the cheap wine they had at the reception. Well, I tell ya, that wine was no cheaper than what I seen Simon drink at home. So that's like the second clue that Simon isn't as rich as he makes out to be."

Sensing that the boy was coming to a conclusion, Chambers said, "Okay..."

"Well, dontcha see it? It's all coming together on the motive side. Oh, damn, and I forgot one thing—Simon knows a bunch of those Portland art dealers! So there it is!" Bradley held out his hands and beamed.

Not sure what to make of all this, Chambers calmly asked, "There what is, Bradley?"

"Jesus, the whole case against Simon!" Bradley burst out, then apologized. "Sorry, sorry, didn't mean to swear. But goddamn it, sir, you see it, don't you?" In an exasperated tone, Bradley said, "So Simon needs money and he knows this Homer painting is worth a pile so he fakes being sick, waits for Jimmy and Thomas to leave, or he goes back right after they leave, then unlocks the back door, steals the painting, loses his key... Maybe he gets all flustered or something... And he doesn't want to get caught so he quick puts the painting in Jimmy's trunk, planning to get it out later on. But then Jimmy gets picked up with the painting in his trunk and Simon just pretends it's all on Jimmy...but it isn't!"

Bradley's theory came out in a tumble and left both himself and Chambers breathless. Chambers's first thought was that he wished he had a friend as loyal as Bradley Little was to Jimmy Park. His second was that perhaps he'd do a little more poking around Simon Britton's finances. His third was that the case possibilities were now expanding rather than contracting. If any part of Bradley's story about Simon's money needs was true, then Simon was looking better and better as the culprit. Still, Chambers couldn't shake his earlier hunch that a

Simon-Jimmy combination could be viable. And now some part of Bradley's story, though Chambers wasn't sure which part, made him wonder if a third possibility was a Bradley-Jimmy scenario. Maybe I ought to just arrest the whole lot of them, he thought, and see who confesses first.

At this point, Jimmy was still on bail as the only official suspect and, on his attorney's advice, he wasn't talking. Simon was looking more and more guilty, and Simon would talk all day, but most of it was claptrap. And now Bradley arrived, cast clear doubt on Simon, but without much to back it up. It all made Chambers wonder if 9:30 AM was too early to go for a long, liquid lunch.

Chapter 18

Choosing to get a cup of coffee rather than an early lunch, Detective Chambers started back to his office when he heard someone call his name. He turned and saw a tall man about his age approaching. Chambers had seen the man around town, knew he was something of an artist—but who in Rascal Harbor wasn't?—and was relieved not to have to come up with a name because the fellow introduced himself. "I'm John McTavish and I think I need to talk with you."

Sensing the man's urgency, Chambers invited him into his office. Sitting in the chair Bradley Little had left no more than 20 minutes earlier, McTavish launched into his story. "I saw Bradley leaving the station as I pulled up and so I'm guessing he came in to see you. And, well, I want you to know that it's probably my fault that he did."

"Oh?"

"Well, yes. You see the boys, Bradley and Jimmy, came over to my cottage last night. They seemed to think that they had put together enough clues to hang Simon Britton as the thief. I don't know how much Bradley told you or if it made any sense. The boy can be a little rash."

"Why don't you tell me what he said last night," Chambers said.

So McTavish related the main details of the discussion—the ink pad falling and the mess it created, Bradley's suspicions about Simon's financial woes and how fencing the painting might solve them. At this last part, and for the second time that morning, Chambers smiled to himself and damned TV detective shows. McTavish continued by unwinding the story about Thomas's, Simon's, and Jimmy's actions after the reception.

"I'm sure you've got your own ideas about the case," McTavish said. "But I guess I wanted you to know that I may have inadvertently encouraged Bradley to come talk with you. Probably a waste of your time."

"No, it wasn't a complete waste of time," Chambers said, still wondering why McTavish was there. "But I thank you for helping me understand why he came in."

McTavish looked relieved and was about to leave when Chambers, sensing an opportunity, said, "If you have a minute, Mr. McTavish, I wonder if we could talk a little more." Settling back into the chair, McTavish nodded. "I haven't been in the Harbor all that long, and I'm still trying to understand the culture and the people. It seems quite different from the place I worked in Florida and what my mother used to describe as life in Aroostook County."

"Coming from northern Maine myself, I'd have to agree with you."

"So I'm wondering if you might fill me in a little about the town in general and the art crowd in particular," Chambers said with a warm smile. "I understand you're an artist yourself."

"Trying to be would be more accurate."

"I admire a man pursuing a dream. So what can you tell me about Robertay Harding, Thomas, Simon, and the like?"

"I'm not sure I'm the best source, I've only moved back full time a short while ago," McTavish said. "My wife and I had a cottage a lot of years and spent summers here but, well, I just moved here, by myself, six months ago."

Chambers nodded, but didn't probe why McTavish was here alone. Instead, he asked, "So you know Robertay and the others?"

"I do, though more from around the fringes than as a full-fledged artist. I've shown some of my work during the open invitations, and I go to the artist shows and receptions. Still, I'm not much of a joiner, and so I see Robertay and Thomas and the Colony folks more from the outside."

"A useful vantage at times."

"Well, anyway…" McTavish continued, sensing that he needed to give the detective something to justify his intrusion. "I expect the Colony folks are like most local art groups—a few folks of decent talent and a lot of wannabes. They can get their backs up about anything and nothing, but when they're agitated, they can be pretty nasty. But mostly I think they're loners, like me, who find the comfort they need in the company of others more or less like themselves."

"That all makes sense, but what about them as individuals?"

"I expect you know that Robertay runs the show around here, has ever since I can remember. Not too many people respect her as an artist, but the old girl runs the Colony efficiently, if with an iron hand, and she's not so full of herself that she can't spot and support new talent. Jimmy Park, for example."

"And Thomas?"

"And Thomas is a lovely guy, pretty good artist at one time, but a little lost these days. I'm not sure that Robertay uses him all that well, but Thomas doesn't seem to mind."

"Could you imagine Robertay ever being involved in any of this mess? Or any of the other Colony board members?" Chambers asked. He didn't think it was likely, but he could see that McTavish had a good eye for people and he really didn't want to deal with the pile of paper on his desk.

"Jesus, I can't imagine so, detective," McTavish said sitting upright. "But then I frankly can't imagine that Jimmy Park did, either. I suppose Simon really does seem like the most obvious candidate, but then he's not sitting in jail so…"

"No, he's not, but that doesn't mean he won't be. Though I'd ask you to keep that to yourself."

McTavish nodded, stood, and turned to leave when Chambers stopped him. "Thanks for coming in, Mr. McTavish, you've given me a couple of things to think about." Handing McTavish his business card, Chambers said, "And if you think of anything else that might be helpful, just give me a call."

"Can't imagine what that would be, but I'll be happy to help if I can."

Chapter 19

McTavish really hadn't helped Chambers, but a piece of paper on his desk did. Realizing he couldn't put off the paperwork, Chambers opened the envelope with the results of the tests he had ordered on the painting and the key. He smiled.

At the garage, Gary half-listened as Louise talked about how tight it was keeping the garage afloat given the money they had had to come up with for Jimmy's bail and how she thought she heard a funny hum in the transmission of the three-year-old Buick Geneva Baxter brought in. "Why don't you stick to the bookkeeping," Gary said with a grumble, a little louder than he meant to. The girl was a crackerjack accountant for his business and a couple others in town. Still, she seemed to spend most of her time poking around the cars in Gary's shop, playing with the various monitors and tools, asking questions, and worse, offering her own conjectures. "Where the hell are you gettin' these ideas from?" he'd demanded at one point.

"The Internet, of course. You can learn anything you want to there."

Julia Nisbett sat in Lydia's front window and almost...almost...regretted giving Caleb Rimes the heave-ho the other day. Caleb had stormed out and threatened not to return until Julia and Trudy apologized. Julia had offered to do so, but Trudy said, "Good god damn, I'm happy to be rid of him and, I think, the boys are, too. He's a crude ass and he smells no better now than he did his last day fishing. To hell with him."

"Thank you, Jesus," Julia wanted to say, but didn't. The thought of apologizing to the lout—and then hearing about it every day for the next year—coiled her stomach. And from what she could tell the table boys were just as glad. Slow Johnston seemed especially pleased as he could now sit at the table with the rest of the fellows no matter what time he came in. Julia suspected that it was the ladies who might have missed Caleb more as his antics, though intolerable, made for good conversation.

Jesus, I oughta write a book, she thought, though I'd have to make it a picture book for the numbnuts in this town.

⁂

Jumper Wilson encountered Ray Manley during a ramble down High Street. This day Jumper's T-shirt read *A penny saved is a penny earned, but it's still just a penny.*

"Jumpah, you got an opinion on this art crime?" Ray asked.

"I do, sir, I do. I think that Homer fella got what he deserved."

"The Homer fella?" asked Ray, forgetting for a moment the name of the artist whose work was stolen. "Why's that, Jumpah?"

"Because if he hadn't gotten all famous, then nobody would of cared if he painted some postcard scene."

"Jesus, never thought about it that way before. So the thief was just doin' everyone a favor?"

"Ayuh," Jumper replied and ambled on.

Nellie Hildreth, looking out the windows of the *Rascal Harbor Gazette* and witnessing the meeting between Jumper and Ray but not the words, looked at the former and thought, I can't wait for that guy to die!

Chapter 20

Chambers continued smiling. After opening the envelope from the state crime lab, he now held in his hands the best lead he had since the Homer watercolor was found in Jimmy Park's trunk. In fact, he had two leads. Thinking back to Jumper Wilson's T-shirt—*Winslow's homer scored two*—his smile broadened.

The leads had a common source—an ink pad of the type that Bradley Little used at the reception. The merest trace of ink from such a pad was embedded alongside a ridge on the key found at the back door of the gallery and a small smudge of the same ink was identified on the back of the Homer painting. Fingerprint analysis was, as Chambers suspected, a wash. There were too many on the watercolor and there were no useable ones—thanks to Constable Kalin—on the key. Chambers had had little in the way of hope when he'd asked Sergeant Levesque to send off both items for testing. "Just following procedures," he'd said when Levesque raised an eyebrow.

Yet sometimes little hopes yield big rewards. And in this instance, Detective Chambers realized that he may have used up every hope-reward relationship he could ever seek. Assuming confirmation that the ink on the key and on the painting was the same as the ink from the pad that Bradley had used, he now had a solid chain of evidence and events that lead in a single direction—to Simon Britton's doorstep.

Chambers was unwilling to abandon the possibility that Jimmy Park, and even Bradley Little, was involved. But when he arrested Simon Britton, Chambers felt he would be able to induce the truth from the artist and wrap up this case.

So Chambers found Chief Miles and laid out the situation. He explained that the ink on the key, undetectable to the eye, had surfaced through a chemical analysis. What turned out to be a smear of the same ink on the back of the painting was clear to anyone who looked. But there were several blots of color on the back—Homer must have been a messy painter, Chambers surmised—and the ink mark only became confirmed when viewed through the crime lab's equipment. Two big clues, then, had surfaced. Combined with Bradley Little's account of the ink pad accident, the ink-based evidence pointed directly toward Simon Britton. Chambers then explained his plan to investigate Britton's financial situation to see if his riches were rumored or true. That Simon's wealth might be less than it seemed was no crime—lots of Rascal Harbor folks inflated or deflated their personal economies based on factors too complex to consider—but if Simon was living beyond his means, it might mean he had a significant motive to steal a small, but valuable painting.

Chief Miles stopped listening as soon as Chambers suggested Simon's name. He wanted Britton arrested upon discovery of the key, but had been persuaded by his detective to hold off until the crime lab report came back. With confirmation of his original hunch, Miles didn't bother to hide his glee at the idea of Simon behind bars. "Now we've got two of 'em!" he said.

Chambers tried to ignore that remark and the one that followed, "Get Arty and go arrest that fairy."

Chambers argued that there was no obvious connection between Simon and Jimmy and that they ought to hold off on arresting Simon until they could confirm the reception night ink pad as the source of the smudges. Miles would not hear of it. "Get Arty and go arrest that fairy!" he repeated. Waiting a beat, he added, "But if it'll make you feel

GEOFFREY SCOTT

better, I'll call up to the lab and get an expedited analysis. Still, I want Britton in a cell today!"

Shrugging, Chambers left the chief's office. He asked Sergeant Levesque to have Officer Kalin round up the ink pad from the gallery—he smiled at the thought of Kalin tangling with Robertay—and to have Officer Long meet Chambers at Simon Britton's house. "I hope this isn't a mistake," he said to himself.

Chapter 21

Simon Britton's arrest lit up the town. Some folks said it was about time—the discovery of Simon's key at the gallery's back door immediately convinced them that he was the real thief. Others held on to the fact that Simon, as a rich man, would have bought the little painting before putting himself at risk by trying to steal it. And still others, likely following Chief Miles's thinking, hoped that a big round up of local artists, especially local gay artists, was just beginning. On this last point, Caleb Rimes was heard to say, "Get 'em all, I say, every last one of the fags," to a small audience at Henry's Barbershop.

When McTavish heard of Rimes's diatribe, he'd been dismayed even if he couldn't say that he was surprised. Mainers can be a funny lot when it comes to folks who walk outside of the mainstream. Many fiercely defend the right of a man—McTavish had only ever heard the phrase, "the right of a *man*"—to do as he pleased as long as it was generally within the limits of the law. The law was the law, but Mainers typically held a fairly liberal definition of its limitations, especially if the law was perceived to infringe on the "right" to do as one pleased. McTavish continued to marvel at instances where a Mainer might, in one breath, damn the "guvment" for trying to stop him from doing "Any goddamn thing I want to do on my property," and then damn a neighbor to hell for posting his land against ATV riders. "I've always rode across that land," the first man would say. "Who's he to tell me I can't?" McTavish sometimes wondered if anyone but himself saw the inherent contradiction in such statements.

Even more confusing were the seemingly unknowable norms around what was considered acceptable in a lifestyle. McTavish had heard every conceivable configuration of human encounter praised… and excoriated. One man might denounce "Them hippies livin' together in the bus down in the cove" to a friend of his while knowing full well that the friend was living as man and wife with two sisters and their assorted children. Similarly, he had witnessed a woman deplore a neighbor for "Trampin' around with every dick in town," and then heap love and attention on the three children her unattached daughter brought home. Those men who had stayed married to the same spouse for 50 years could be ridiculed as mercilessly as those women who were on their third and fourth husbands; kids of a second marriage could cast stones at their step-siblings from a third; and those who dallied outside of a sanctioned marriage could be upheld or upbraided depending, apparently, on the phase of the moon.

But all of this moral meandering went into hyper-drive when it came to gay folks. Mainers could be, by turns, the most tolerant and the least biased, and the most narrow-minded and the least accepting of gays that McTavish had ever seen. Some gay couples found themselves widely embraced and their lifestyle conveniently ignored, while others were explicitly ignored because their lifestyle would never be embraced.

"See, this is why I don't care about people's social lives," McTavish had said to Maggie years ago in person and to her now in spirit. "It's nonsensical. If they would just listen to themselves, half these folks would die of embarrassment." Maggie, whose tolerance for all things absurd included her husband, tried to explain "the flaw" of human existence. McTavish listened, he really did, but he could only accept her argument until the next time he encountered an instance of "the flaw."

Witnessing bizarre or biased or byzantine words, actions, or both, McTavish would roll his eyes if alone or roll his eyes and say "See?" if Maggie was near. With Maggie gone, McTavish found himself even less tolerant of "the flaw" and worried that his eye rolling might lead to blindness.

And so, in Simon's arrest, the Rascal Harbor residents saw whatever it was that each of them wanted to see. Most hoped that it meant a final resolution to the case; a fair-sized minority, however, had enjoyed the fracas too much to be happy about it drawing to a close.

Chapter 22

That latter group needn't have worried: Simon's arrest produced nothing like the quick resolution that Chief Miles, Detective Chambers, and most of the town folks sought. After burbling, mewling, and outright crying during the arrest, Simon took his lawyer's advice and refused to talk. The town had a new and more viable culprit, but still no finality.

The availability of news on satellite radio, cable television, and the Internet had savaged the sales of daily newspapers. Subscriptions to weeklies like the *Rascal Harbor Gazette* had also fallen, but by a smaller percentage. One reason was that, because their circulations never came close to those of their big city peers, they had fewer customers to lose. Another reason was that weeklies reported the kinds of things that larger papers, television, and most radio stations ignored. Store grand openings, selectman battles, school graduations, and local sports defined the weeklies' world and so residents looked to papers like the *Gazette* for their community news and opinion. Finally, weeklies survived and sometimes flourished because folks wanted to see what their friends and neighbors thought about pressing issues. So it was often the case that the letters to the editor section of a good weekly newspaper dwarfed the column inches given to actual news.

All of these reasons and more—most notably Nellie Hildreth's must-read obituaries—meant that the *Gazette*'s circulation remained steady…and profitable. Every local hotel, restaurant, and tourist shop advertised, but the ads for the antique sales, shows, and festivals could nearly pay the paper's expenses by themselves. Nellie and her staff often marveled at how much junk could be sold, resold, and then driven to the town landfill. "Advertising all that old shit keeps us in business," Nellie would say. "Sure hope folks keep digging it up."

Sarah McAdams, the one full-time reporter Nellie could afford—and the only one who she had ever liked—was tiring of reports on flower shows, retirement parties, and guest speakers at the ladies clubs. She sensed a chance to make a name for herself through stories about the theft. Sarah had finished three years of a journalism degree before a short romance lead to a long pregnancy and the birth of her daughter Clara. Without the means to finance herself and a baby and college tuition bills, Sarah moved back to Rascal Harbor and the house in which she came of age. It wasn't a bad life. Her mother, recently widowed, adored Clara. Sarah liked her co-workers at the *Gazette*; and, after a couple set-tos, had created a working relationship with Nellie that they both could abide. Still, she dreamed of a big piece and the chance to take her skills to a bigger venue.

And so she dug into the Simon Britton story. Of course, she'd dug into the Jimmy Park arrest as well, but, other than the discovery of the painting in the Park kid's trunk, there wasn't a whole lot to report. Simon Britton's arrest, however, brought all kinds of dynamics to bear.

Sarah's account of Simon's apprehension filled the first half of the story; reaction to and commentary on it filled the rest. McTavish, who usually turned first to Nellie's obituaries, found himself caught up in Sarah McAdams's narrative:

Britton Arrested for Theft

On Tuesday, October 15, Detective Richard Chambers and Officer Arthur Long arrested Simon Britton, age 55, at his home on Oak Street. On advice of his attorney, Britton refused to talk with police, Detective Chambers said. Britton's attorney, Paul Reny from Portland, said his client was "completely innocent of the charge" and intended to plead not guilty at his arraignment scheduled for Wednesday.

Britton was charged with Class B Theft. Maine criminal statutes define theft as "obtaining or exercising unauthorized control over the property of another with intent to deprive the other person of the property." Because the stolen Winslow Homer painting is valued at more than $10,000, Britton is accused of a Class B crime. If convicted, Britton could be incarcerated in the Maine Department of Corrections for up to 10 years and be fined up to $20,000. According to Portland art dealer, Edward Zimmer, the Homer painting could probably sell for $100,000 or more at auction.

"The evidence against Mr. Britton is solid," Detective Chambers said. "First, his key to the back door of the Colony art gallery was found at the scene. Second, that key had a trace of the same ink pad ink that was used to mark the guests at the reception for the Homer painting. Third, a smudge of the same ink was identified on the back of the painting. And finally, Simon Britton is the only person to have had that ink on his fingers. All other guests had the ink stamped on the backs of their hands."

Continuing, Detective Chambers said, "We are investigating other leads related to Mr. Britton's finances and his whereabouts at the time of the theft."

Asked if Britton's arrest means that the charges will be dropped against James Park, who was arrested soon after the theft was discovered, Detective Chambers said, "No. We still consider Mr. Park a suspect."

County District Attorney, Lee Turcotte, echoed Detective Chambers's summary. "We will continue to investigate all angles of this crime, but we feel that our case against Simon Britton is a strong one," he said.

Chief Miles praised the work of the entire Rascal Harbor police department for its work on the case. He singled out Officer Rendall Kalin for his work in finding the back-door key, which Miles claimed launched the investigation in a new direction and lead to Simon Britton's arrest. "The people of Rascal Harbor are well served every day by the brave members of the police department. They put their lives on the line to protect the town from people like Simon Britton and James Park," the chief added.

Townspeople had mixed reactions to the arrest. Robertay Harding, President of the Rascal Harbor Art Colony board, released a statement saying, "It saddens me that this tragic situation has come to our lovely little town. I am pleased that the case may soon be resolved, though I am dismayed that one of our own might really be the offender."

Minerva Williams, former cafeteria worker at the Rascal Harbor Elementary School, said, "I don't know who did it, can't say I really care. But I don't like it that Jimmy Park is still under suspicion. He's a good boy and they ought to just let him be."

Bill Candlewith, a retired long-liner, added, "Well, it's been quite a thing here in town. It's got lots of folks' tongues wagging. We don't have too many robberies here in the Harbor. Guess it's a good thing they found the guy this time."

Technically, the Art Colony crime was a theft rather than a robbery. A robbery is the forcible taking of another person's property by violence or through fear.

With his arrest, Britton now faces arraignment at which time Superior Court Judge Kenneth Langston will review the charges and ask for a plea. Bail can also be requested during the arraignment. Judge Langston may also set a date for a preliminary hearing during which probable cause to make a formal charge will be determined.

Though he refused to be interviewed for this story, local resident Jumper Wilson has been wearing a T-shirt that seems to sum up many people's views: *Facts are facts, but the truth stinks.*

McTavish had picked up the *Gazette* on his way to Lydia's and he finished the McAdams story as he finished his first molasses donut. About to turn to the obituaries, he tuned in to the rising voices of the men at the back table. They, too, had been reading the report and found much to analyze.

"Bill, you dumbass, everybody knows the difference between theft and robbery!" Vance Edwards began. "Christ, even Slow knows." Slow Johnston, still reading the story, looked up, and smiled.

"Slow don't know shit," replied Candlewith. "And it was an honest mistake. Hell, I got a little flusterated with that reporter girl and her tape recorder."

"The tape recorder or 'that reporter girl'?" asked Ray Manley. "She is kinda cute."

"Ray, that girl is young enough to be your granddaughter," Rob Pownall said.

"But she ain't my granddaughter and I ain't dead," Ray replied.

At that point, a cackle came from the ladies' table and Minerva Williams's voice boomed, "Jesus, you might as well be, you old coot. Ray, your roosterin' days are long gone!"

"But your hen-peckin' days are still upon us. I don't know how Russell puts up with you," Ray replied, to guffaws at the men's table and scoffs at the ladies'.

"You best watch yourself, old Ray," Minerva said in warning. "Someone might come around and *robbery* you of the family jewels!"

"All right, all right," Trudy said, jumping into the conversation. "Jesus, you all settle yourselves down. This isn't a goddamn playground."

A chorus of "Sorry, Trudy" rumbled across the back of the restaurant while barely concealed snickers tittered across the front. McTavish smiled and turned to the obituaries. Today, "the flaw" struck him as humorous indeed.

Chapter 23

McTavish was still smiling about "the flaw" when he realized that he'd missed a call from his son, Noah. "Damn, I haven't heard word one from the boy in months and now I miss his call," he said to himself. McTavish hit redial, waited as it rang, and then swore to himself when Noah's voicemail came on.

"Ah, sorry, Son…ah…I guess I missed your call, so I'm calling you back," McTavish said, fumbling over the words. "Give me a call when you have a chance."

Though he tried not to read too much into the missed call—after all, it could have been a butt dial—McTavish kept twisting it around in his mind. Later in the day, he tried and failed to remember the last time they had spoken on the phone. They had seen each other at Maggie's funeral, but McTavish couldn't actually recall talking with Noah after that.

He heard Maggie in his head, "Jesus, John, what kind of father doesn't even remember the last time he's talked to his son?" The answer came in both his voice and Maggie's. "The kind that doesn't even know how to act toward his son at his mother's funeral."

And with that thought, McTavish's mind reeled. He knew that he had stumbled through Maggie's death and its aftermath. Noah was around, but so were a house full of Maggie's friends and family and McTavish relatives, and the hours and days seemed to swirl in ways that turned everything to mush. Some memories now came as shards—sharp edged and clear—but he couldn't get them to cohere, the pieces just didn't seem to fit. And hanging over the few clear images that he had was a light, gray memory haze. People, events, and places moved into and around in shadows, almost discernible, but not quite, almost comforting, but not really. McTavish sensed that he handled it okay, that he hadn't embarrassed Maggie or himself, but he also felt that people were watching and waiting and wondering about him.

He hadn't cried. That was one thing McTavish knew people were concerned about—"Have you cried, John?" "It's okay to cry." "Crying might help." Their words were offered in all sincerity; McTavish knew they meant well and knew that they might even be right. But he hadn't cried, hadn't broken down head in hands shaking all over as he had seen in the movies. He had showered and shaved, accepted condolences, and eaten the food that arrived in armloads—he'd done the things that people do, outwardly at least. But it was his public self that did all this, the confident, if self-effacing self that could lecture in front of 50 undergraduates, present a new course proposal in front of 15 department colleagues, and make a presentation in front of hundreds of conference session participants.

But it was a front. McTavish's at-the-core-of-his-being self was shy, quiet, observant, kind…and distant. College teaching made him realize that he could have another self; Maggie helped him see a third. Eventually, he realized that he had others as well. Son, brother, father—each of these selves, Maggie had said, were part and parcel of the John McTavish that she loved. None were completely independent, each drew on attributes of the others. "That's how you get to be a whole person, John," Maggie said.

A big part of McTavish's brain could accept this idea, that each of us is both one and many. But in dour moments he couldn't shake the feeling that he was nothing more than a series of fronts—clear, but shallow images of someone who looked like him, and who people saw and reacted to. But these were singular and shallow images rather than a true and complete whole.

McTavish had never voiced these ideas, even to Maggie. He'd thought about doing so several times, even started to once or twice. In the end, however, he'd pulled back for fear that he wouldn't make sense, that he needed more time to think it through, that he'd feel too vulnerable if he put words to his feelings. He didn't know or understand his reticence, but he followed its lead.

Of course, Maggie could read him like no one else; she knew all about his reticence. She'd come to accept it on some levels, but she felt comfortable pushing him, if gently, to open up, "Come on, John. I know you've got feelings and I know you can talk. Put the two together."

He typically smiled, shrugged, and said, "Once I get it worked out, Mags, I'll spill like a weathered old dam." Then he'd give her a hug and promise himself that he really would try to figure it all out. In the meantime, however, there were always other things to think about.

McTavish came honestly by his reserved nature. Combined with what Maggie called "That big sigh of yours," however, it had not helped his relationship with Noah. He loved the boy, as much or more than he loved Maggie. But loving someone and knowing how to interact with him can be two very different things.

McTavish's own father had been a hard man to know. He wasn't mean or aggressive or even unkind; he'd been quiet, inwardly focused, and hard working. He'd talked sparingly and his talk focused on work. McTavish's mother talked more and about a greater range of topics, but feelings in the McTavish family were to be felt rather than discussed. McTavish and his siblings sensed their parents' care and concern and even love. But those feelings were expressed through their presence, through the food and shelter and guidance they provided, and through a largely unspoken encouragement to do one's best. Words, not so much.

As a father, then, McTavish had provided a similar presence for Noah. He'd expected the boy to draw the same strength and security from him that he had from his father. But it hadn't worked. The boy needed more, and McTavish had no idea how to offer it. In fact, when he tried, his words of incentive seemed more likely to irritate than to encourage the boy. It was Maggie who held them together and, with her death, their tenuous bond cracked.

At least it did until this day when McTavish's phone had rung and he'd missed the call from his son. He wasn't sure he was ready to be all the things a widowed father needed to be for his child, but he felt a duty to try.

As he reached for the Bushmills, McTavish felt the phone ring in his pocket. It was Noah. "I've got a fall break and I wondered if I might come to the cottage."

Flustered, McTavish said, "Well…sure, I'm here now full-time and so…"

"I know, I know. They close down the dorms during this break and I thought I could go to my roommate's house, but his parents are having trouble, and, well I—"

"No, I mean…of course…yes, you can always come, you know, when you're not in class." McTavish stopped for fear of saying something else dumb and off-putting.

They worked out that Noah would fly to Portland the next week and McTavish would pick him up for a three-day visit. As they hung up, McTavish heard Maggie's voice, "This is an opportunity, John, do something with it."

Chapter 24

A calm followed Simon Britton's arrest and that meant a change in the table talk at Lydia's. Rumors still floated through, but none inspired much interest among either the men or women. Talk never stops at a local diner, however, it just drifts in different directions.

Or it did until Ray Manley brought the news that Detective Chambers had identified some significant issues with Simon's monetary affairs. Ray had gotten this information from Caleb Rimes who had learned it from Constable Kalin who had pieced it together from inquiries he'd overheard the chief detective make. Normally the one to make such announcements, and to make them loudly, Caleb had not returned to Lydia's and so was spreading his news at other Harbor outlets where the curious congregated.

Still burned by his last diner encounter with Minerva, Ray brought this intelligence to the boys sotto voce. The ladies noticed the quiet whispers that accompanied Ray's arrival, but years of loud children and loud jobs had dulled their ears such that they would have had a hard time listening in if they tried.

The ladies had an unwitting ally, however. Ray's report and the boys' conversation had progressed no more than five minutes when Slow Johnston's voice boomed out, "What did you say about Simon's flannels?"

"Jesus, Slow, I said his 'financials,'" Ray said loud enough for the girls to hear. "And keep your goddamned voice down!"

"Hell, no need to now, Ray Manley," Minerva said and cackled. "Slow's let the herring out of the net and they're headed back out to sea!"

The boys released a collective sigh, Vance Edwards cuffed Slow on the head and said, "Slow, by Jesus, I'm gonna weld you a new ear. Maybe even two of 'em."

"Might as well weld him up a new brain while you're at it," Ray said, sputtering.

"Oh, you boys leave Slow alone," Maude Anderson said. "You know he's got a bad ear."

"And he ain't the only one with a bad brain over at that table," Minerva added.

"Enough!" yelled Julia and Trudy at the same time. "Go back to your corners, mop up the blood, and get ready for Round Two somewhere else," Trudy continued. Looking at Julia, Trudy added, "Christ, they're no better than seven-year-olds."

Trudy's outburst sparked the tablemates to check the time and decide that the coffee hour was over. As they filtered away, however, Geraldine Smythe pulled Rob Pownall aside and got the scoop on the investigation into Simon's finances and the added incentive they seemed to indicate for his role in the theft. Geraldine thought about waiting until the next day to bring her friends up to speed, but decided it couldn't wait—after all, once Geneva Baxter got the news it would be everywhere, even if all wrong. So she called each of them in turn and offered up a succinct account knowing that, by tomorrow, they'd all have worked their sources and the emerging story would be standing on a set of steady legs.

Detective Chambers walked into Lydia's about ten minutes after the back-table crews had left. Had he arrived earlier, he might have been cornered and given the Rascal Harbor version of the third degree. Instead, he picked up a cup of coffee to go and was about to leave when Trudy pulled him aside.

"Just to let you know, detective, the word's out that you're investigating Simon's financial situation and that it's not looking good for him," Trudy said quietly.

"Oh?"

"Hell, you know what small towns are like," Trudy continued. "Someone gets a nugget of information, makes all kinds of assumptions, and then the thing's like a lit match."

"Got it. I expect I know who that someone might be."

"I expect you do," Trudy said with a shake of her head. "I expect you do. Though guess you can't arrest 'someone' for being a moron."

"Need a whole lot more jail cells if we did," Chambers replied with a grin.

"Agreed," Trudy said with a mock smile. "But then what would folks do for entertainment around here?" Trudy hesitated, then looked at Chambers directly and said softly, "Leastwise they ain't talking about you and that Ludlow gal."

Chambers's eyes widened and Trudy snorted. "Thought you might have an unexamined life, eh, detective? Not around the Harbor!" Trudy then went on to give a short account of where and when Chambers and Toni Ludlow had been seen, though she refused to say who had done the spying. "Small town eyes and ears, they're always open, Dick. Especially for a single man of means and one who doesn't smell like a bait trap."

Chambers knew that Trudy was having some fun at his expense, but he liked her and trusted that she might be a valuable ally in time. So he smiled sheepishly, shook his head subtly, said, "You're the tops, Trudy," and left.

CHAPTER 25

Chambers returned to the station more shaken by Trudy's second revelation than her first. Apparently his attempt to meet with Toni Ludlow was clumsier than he thought. Best to cool that budding relationship now, he thought, until after this case is settled.

She would understand, Chambers hoped. After all, he'd been upfront about the possibility of town talk and thus their one date—Chambers felt funny even using the word—had been dinner at a small Italian place 25 miles up the coast. Rascal Harbor tongues travel a long way, he thought as he wondered who might have seen them. That they did and that the news had reached at least Trudy's ears meant that he was busted. He made a note on his desk blotter to give Toni a call later in the day.

With his relationship possibilities on hold, Chambers turned with greater urgency to his investigation into Simon Britton's finances. He had made considerable progress to date and had only a few details to nail down. The fact that Simon Britton had not been able to post sufficient surety for bail was a good indicator that he had money troubles. A strong financial motive combined with the other pieces of evidence were adding up to a convincing case to convict Britton of the theft.

That Chambers could not find a clear connection between Britton and Jimmy Park bothered him. He had dismissed the possibility of a link to Bradley Little; the boy didn't seem stable enough to be an able crime partner. But the painting was found in Park's trunk and, though he hated to admit it, Chambers could not shake the idea that Britton and Park could be lovers as well as thieves. Yet, with neither of them talking and no evidence to speak of, it was more idea than reality.

To pursue the latter, Chambers put in a call to District Attorney Lee Turcotte. Chambers knew that Turcotte had doubts that Jimmy Park was involved. With the painting in Parks's trunk, Turcotte had to arraign the boy, but his own investigations into the matter left him skeptical of Parks's guilt. Chambers also knew that Turcotte despised Chief Miles and knew all about his ill-disguised bias against gays. If we push Britton, maybe we can clear or convict Parks, Chambers thought as he dialed Turcotte's number.

So that was the pitch that Chambers made to Turcotte: Let's press Britton hard on an accomplice and see if he'll roll on Parks for a better deal. Turcotte agreed and said he would set it up a meeting with Britton through his lawyer.

※

Chambers had seen a lot of suspects crumble after their first jail stay, but he was surprised at how bad Simon Britton looked as he shuffled into the meeting room with his lawyer. Haggard only began to describe Britton's appearance. From head to toe, the man seemed deflated, as if his body was shrinking into itself. It was Britton's face that Chambers focused on, however, for the dull eyes, disheveled hair, and poorly shaved cheeks signaled a man who had lost most of his reserve.

Chambers felt badly. Although he knew that jail could take the starch out of most men, Chambers knew that it went especially badly for gay men. Any advances the greater society had made in understanding alternative lifestyles died at the jailhouse door. A first-time stay was bad enough for anyone; it had clearly struck Simon Britton full force.

But Chambers also knew that Britton's time behind bars was likely to play well in the search for an accomplice. His last interrogation had gone nowhere as Britton's lawyer simply reminded his client that he need not say a word. During that meeting, Simon had been upset, crying and burbling, and incoherent whenever he did speak. Still, he hadn't been jail crushed at that point and, like it or not, Chambers expected Britton would see a benefit in being more forthcoming now.

"I can't imagine what you think this meeting will accomplish," Britton's lawyer, Paul Reny, said. "You've incarcerated an innocent man who is suffering the travails of jail life. So unless you are here to tell us that he's being released immediately, then I see no purpose—"

"Just hold on, councilor," Turcotte said. "Save your indignation for the courtroom. We're here to talk about some possibilities that could help your client."

Simon, who had acknowledged neither Turcotte nor Chambers, continued to sit with unfocused eyes staring at the tabletop. Reny leaned back, crossed his arms, and nodded to Turcotte. "All right, let's hear what you have to say."

As they had discussed, Turcotte turned to Chambers who, in his kindest voice, said Simon's name. Getting no response, Chambers repeated Simon's name, "Simon, we know you're having a rough time in jail. It's not a nice place to be. District Attorney Turcotte thinks he can do something about that if you'll cooperate—"

Reny jumped in. "Simon, you are an innocent man and you need not say a word that incriminates you."

Chambers continued as if he'd not heard Reny. "Simon, we have a mound of evidence against you so we're not here today to talk about your innocence or guilt." Chambers said these last words looking directly at Reny. "What we are here to discuss is your accomplice. James Park had the Homer painting in his car trunk. You've said you didn't put it there, so it must have been the Park boy. Help us help you, Simon. Tell us about Park's involvement."

Britton gave no indication that he had heard Chambers's pitch.

District Attorney Turcotte waited a minute, then focused the incentive. "Mr. Britton, if you cooperate in naming your accomplice, then I may be able to get the judge to reduce your bail to an amount that would mean you could soon be home. And if you do that and you confess to the crime, then I will argue for a lighter sentence. I can't make any promises mind you, but I'll do everything that I can."

As Chambers, and then Turcotte spoke, Simon continued to stare at the table. Halfway through, he began shaking his head and mumbling, "No." When Turcotte finished, Simon looked up for the first time. Though his face was still gaunt, Simon's eyes registered a new spark. Looking directly at Chambers, Britton said, "I told you, detective, that I was not involved in this theft. I'm telling you now that, as far as I know, James Park was not either. He could not be my accomplice as I committed no crime." The effort to muster these words seemed to take whatever strength Britton had for he sagged back into his seat and set his eyes back on the table.

"You men are making a terrible mistake in keeping my client locked up on a false charge," Paul Reny said. "Your evidence is all circumstantial and you know it."

"Circumstantial evidence is still evidence, councilor," Turcotte replied. "Look, we're trying to help your client get out of here. He's accused of a very serious crime and the mounting evidence all points in his direction. So don't let your notions about the legal definitions of evidence cloud your duty to your client—"

"All right you two, enough," Chambers said. Turning to Simon, he said softly, "Simon, if James Park was not your accomplice, are you saying that you committed the crime alone? If that's the case, then do what's right so that the kid can get on with his life."

Whatever reserve Simon displayed earlier was gone. The hollow man who now looked at Chambers simply shook his head. "I won't say what is untrue," he said and lowered his eyes again.

Chambers and Turcotte looked at one another as if to say, "What the hell does that mean?" Paul Reny, sensing their confusion, stood up,

GEOFFREY SCOTT

helped Simon to his feet, and said, "We're done here." Reny knocked on the door to call the guard, and then walked his client out.

The detective and the district attorney stayed seated and stayed looking at one another. "Did he mean that it was untrue that he committed the crime, that the Park kid was not his accomplice, or both?" asked Turcotte.

"Damned if I know."

"Well, we've got to figure out something. I can't keep putting off the probable cause hearing for Jimmy Park. And at this point, the only reasons he's not been cleared are the painting in his trunk and Chief Miles's prejudice. We've got no witnesses, we've got no fingerprints. If I don't get something else, then Judge Langston will throw the case out. And I could hardly blame him."

"You know as well as I do that all the evidence points toward Simon Britton," said Chambers calmly. "We thought this little meeting might shake Simon up enough to get him some leniency by naming his conspirator. We've got no confession and we're as confused as ever about Jimmy Park's involvement. You're right, however: If we had to go to court today, the judge would take us for idiots."

"Then you'd better start prepping your chief for that possibility, detective, because unless you find something in the next day or two, I'm going to let the charges drop."

Turcotte didn't see it, but Chambers felt a finger of dread work up his spine at the thought of approaching Chief Miles with this news. It wasn't that he feared the chief—he knew the man to be more bluster than beef. Instead, he feared losing his temper at the chief's likely ignorant and petulant response. He'd come to like living in this town and he didn't want to think about uprooting should he smack his chief on the jaw. Be mighty satisfying though, he thought.

Chambers and Turcotte shook hands and left the jail. As they parted, however, Chambers thought, wonder how long it will be before the news of this meeting makes it to Lydia's.

Chapter 26

John McTavish heard the news one day later, though not from the back-table folks at Lydia's. Instead Gary Park called him that afternoon and asked if he could come by the house as "Something's up with the case against Jimmy." McTavish had just miscut a piece of trim so he was happy to take a break.

As McTavish walked through the kitchen door, Gary handed him a tumbler half full of Bushmills. "Come in, John, come in," Gary said, clearly excited.

"Where's Ruby?" McTavish asked. If both Gary and Ruby were going to tell the story, McTavish knew that he'd need to pay close attention as the double-barreled narrative was likely to meander.

"She's over at Charlotte's gettin' her hair reattached," Gary said. Ruby had androgenic alopecia, the female equivalent of male pattern baldness. She'd worn wigs of various hues for the last five years, but had recently discovered hair extensions. According to Gary, Ruby had "About a thousand of 'em glued or clamped or sewed into her head." McTavish doubted the accuracy of this description, but he didn't doubt the outcome—Ruby did indeed have a full head of rust-colored hair, a color that managed to look both artificial and appropriate at the same time. The problem was that Charlotte Givens, proprietress and chief stylist at Charlotte's Hair, was nearly blind. At Ruby's last appointment, the extensions Charlotte wove into Ruby's hair were mostly of the same hue, but there were a couple bright red pieces showing on the back of Ruby's head. That these pieces were three inches longer than the rest contributed to the carnival-like look. Ruby couldn't see the back of her head, of course, so she was happy.

With Ruby engaged, McTavish thought he might get the story from Gary, and then be on his way. "So what's going on?"

"Well, got a call from Julian. Seems he got a call from Simon's lawyer. He and Simon had some meeting with the police and district attorney. Guess they wanted Simon to roll over on Jimmy. They was danglin' a carrot—tell 'em Jimmy helped him steal that paintin' and he'd get a lighter sentence."

"But that would only work if Simon was guilty."

"Course, but they're figurin' that the evidence is so strong against him that he'll see the writin' on the wall and cave."

"So how did it go?"

"Simon's lawyer tells Julian that Simon's in real bad shape. Jail ain't no place for a guy like Simon a'course. But when those guys pushed him, Simon gets himself together and tells 'em flat out that he ain't guilty and neither is Jimmy."

"Okay…" McTavish said, still trying to understand if there was anything new here.

"Well, so here's the thing, Simon's lawyer tells Julian that he can't see how they can keep Jimmy on the string. They got him for having the paintin' in his trunk, but everything else says that Simon did it. Julian actually thinks they might let Jimmy go!"

"'Let Jimmy go,' as in they might not bring formal charges?"

"Right, right," said Gary, showing the first hint of weak smile. "Maybe, just maybe this goddamn mess will be over soon."

"Over for Jimmy, maybe, but sounds like Simon's still in a fix."

"Well, if he done it, then he should be, and damn him for getting Jimmy involved by puttin' that paintin' in his trunk."

"Fair enough."

"Fair huff?" Ruby said as she entered the kitchen. "Who's dat in a fair huff and what's de huff all about?" McTavish knew that Ruby's relationship to the English language often teetered toward nonsense, but he suspected some actual deafness was a contributing factor.

"Nobody's in a huff, Ruby," Gary said and sighed.

"Good, cause if John's in a huff then hell's gonna get the ice cubes." Gary sighed again. "Freeze over, Ruby, hell's gonna freeze over."

"Well, I hope so. Dat way the devil he gonna be havin' a cloudy day!" Ruby giggled as she trailed off to the living room.

As she did, McTavish turned to Gary and said, "Ahhhh....looks like Charlotte turned her calendar ahead an extra month again." He nodded toward the back of Ruby's departing head where they saw that Charlotte had added both green and red extensions throughout Ruby's hair. "Christ, she's looks like a Christmas tree! All we need's some twinkly lights and we can put presents under her!"

McTavish smiled, but added no comment as he knew that no one but Gary could point out Ruby's eccentricities. Proof of that particular pudding was the name patch on Gary's work shirts. Ruby had ordered them over the phone. Apparently the letters "y" and "i" sound a bit too alike to her hearing-challenged ears. So when she insisted that she wanted the name to be spelled "Gari," the clerk complied and Gary now had a dozen such shirts. He wore one every day and grumbled when he did so. Still, he would brook not a single word of criticism toward Ruby and woe came to anyone who crossed that particular line.

"So what's next?" McTavish asked, returning to the subject at hand.

"Oh right, so Julian thinks the DA is going to fold and not bring the charges and Jimmy will be free."

"Fingers crossed."

"Fingers crossed is money in the bank" Ruby called out.

Hmmm, McTavish thought, maybe Ruby's hearing isn't her biggest problem.

CHAPTER 27

Noah arrived the next day. McTavish picked him up at the Portland Airport and, after an awkward embrace and the typical exchange about the trip, they headed north to Rascal Harbor.

If asked, McTavish would have admitted having mixed feelings about Noah's visit. He was happy to see his son, he really was. But he knew that they needed to talk in ways and about things that he didn't know if he could handle…or handle very well. Hope I don't screw this up, he kept saying to himself. In his ear, Maggie said, "I hope you don't either, John."

McTavish wondered if Noah, too, felt uneasy. The boy sat quietly as they drove through the Portland traffic. McTavish suspected that Noah shared Maggie's capacity for baring his feelings rather than McTavish's own disposition to bury them. So he braced himself for "the talk."

Outside the city, Noah surprised him by asking about the theft of the Homer painting. McTavish had mentioned it during their last phone call and apparently the boy had later looked up the details online. He seemed curious, so McTavish extended his narrative in hopes that the story would last until they arrived at the cottage.

It almost did. Noah listened attentively, if quietly. The few questions he raised were smart and generally beyond what McTavish knew.

He seemed more interested in the people, however, than in the crime itself—what was Simon's standing in the community, why hadn't Jimmy come out as a gay man, how had Robertay Harding remained the head of the Art Colony? None of these questions had occurred to McTavish, and he stumbled as he tried to answer them. Still, he smiled to himself as he thought, good Lord, we're having a conversation. He could almost see Maggie smiling in his mind's eye.

At the cottage, Noah walked around as if remembering a place once visited in a dream. He moved slowly, stopping often to look at a picture or to pick up an object. McTavish watched without speaking knowing that he would approach this place the same way. Noah's face betrayed little and McTavish couldn't tell if he was happy to be there or not.

"You've done some work," Noah said as he joined his father in a kitchen rocking chair. "It looks a lot like it did when I was here last, but you've made some changes."

"I suppose I have."

"I can still feel Mom's presence though and that's a good thing, her needlepoint pictures and her shell collection, even her knitting basket is in the same place. I wondered if you'd get rid of all that stuff."

"Why would I do that?" McTavish felt surprised by the comment.

"Well, you never liked all the stuff she collected—I remember you called it 'clutter.' It was a funny word to me so I always remembered it and, well, Mom did like to collect stuff. But I'm surprised to see it all still here. I guess….I guess…I just figured you wanted to withdraw after she died and so having her stuff around would be an annoyance."

"An annoyance?" McTavish asked. He couldn't believe Noah was saying these things. He admitted that he had been annoyed, at times, by Maggie's acquisitive disposition. Maggie drew comfort from having material things around her that spoke of home and hearth—cloth for sewing projects, baskets for decorating projects, yarn for knitting projects—and shells. Whenever they stayed at the cottage, Maggie collected shells. She had no systematic approach; she seemed uninterested in trying to collect samples of various categories. Maggie just liked looking for and bringing home shells that struck her as "interesting."

"Where are you, Dad? You sorta drifted off."

"I suppose I did. Just thinking about all the stuff your mother accumulated." McTavish paused. "And you're right. I suppose I did think of it as clutter at the time. But I haven't thought about it since I moved back. Not even sure that I really see it anymore. I guess it keeps her alive for me."

"Jesus, Dad, did you just express a feeling? You haven't gone all soft and squishy have you?" As McTavish looked at him, Noah continued. "You know it would have been nice if you'd shown some feelings when she was alive."

Ah, Christ, McTavish thought, guess we're going to do "the talk" now.

"She loved you entirely, you know," Noah said. "And somehow she knew that you loved her. But it sure wasn't obvious. Wasn't obvious to me anyway. I mean you were always there. You weren't off playing golf or poker or drinking at the bar with your buddies—did you even have any buddies? You were there, but it was like you weren't there either. 'A silent presence'—one of Mom's friends gave me a book about grief with that title—that's you, Dad. A silent presence."

McTavish knew he ought to challenge some of this characterization. He had feelings, for Christ's sake; he wasn't made of ice. As Noah talked, McTavish was continually struck by how much the boy was his mother. Maggie could strike exactly the same tone—soft-glove critique. Maggie had never shied from pointing out McTavish's faults, but she'd always done so with a heart that he knew loved him. Noah's criticism seemed a little sharper than Maggie's. But Maggie had had years of practice and much fodder to practice on. McTavish would hear the boy out without biting back.

"You drifted off again there, Dad. Kind of hard to have a conversation with you when you're only half there."

STEALING HOMER

"You're right, Noah," McTavish said. "Guess I'm just struck by how much you remind me of your mother…and it takes me aback." Sensing that his son wanted more, McTavish hesitated, then said, "I loved your mother, Noah, and…well, I love you."

"'Well, I love you'…? Jesus, Dad, you say that like it's the hardest thing in the world! I just don't understand! Why can't you just say what you feel?" Noah's eyes reddened. "I just don't get you!" He hesitated, then said, "It was just so much easier with Mom." Noah got up from his chair, opened the kitchen door, and walked out.

"It was, Maggie," McTavish said just loud enough for himself to hear it. "You made it easier."

McTavish put the newspaper down and sat rocking for a while. His mind filled with all manner of memory—happy and sad, noteworthy and mundane, six months and six years ago. It was as if someone had turned on a memory machine and set the dial to "random." Some memories were of his university job and the family's Midwestern home; other thoughts were of Noah and ball games and birthday parties; but most of the images were of Maggie and, of those, most featured Maggie's smile. It had been some time since he'd seen Maggie's generous, open, welcoming smile, the gesture that so clearly defined her. She'd tried to smile during her last months, sometimes almost succeeding. Her efforts fooled most of her friends, but they never fooled McTavish. He knew the real Maggie, his Maggie, was slipping from him. He couldn't make it stop nor could he figure out how to fill the hole that slippage left. He was still a man—smart, capable, artistic, and handy. With Maggie, however, he'd been a *better* man.

Noah returned fifteen minutes later to find his father still rocking in his kitchen chair. He took down a couple of glasses and filled them with ice. He found the Bushmills bottle and poured two inches into one glass, half of that amount into the other. To the second, he added a generous amount of water. He handed the first glass to his dad and sat down with the other. They clicked glasses silently, then Noah said, "Well, there's always the Irish."

The McTavishes passed the supper hour with a meal of steak and French fries. No salads or vegetables for these two as Maggie had been the only one pushing healthy choices. Each smiled inwardly as he sat down to eat and saw nothing green dotting his plate. Though neither spoke, each heard Maggie's whisper, "Jesus, you two!" and secretly pledged to do better...next time.

The talk was of school—McTavish's questions about Noah's studies and friends, and Noah's questions about whether McTavish missed his university life.

The latter was a shorter conversation. "Not as much as I might have expected," McTavish said. "I still think about another book or two, but my ambitions are running more toward art these days."

"Don't you miss your colleagues and the students?"

"Again, not as much as I might have expected. I hear from some of them over email and I let them know that I'm doing fine. Some say that they'll visit, but I really don't expect them to."

McTavish kept deflecting the conversation back to Noah's classes. Noah was a junior at a Big Ten university, much larger than the one at which McTavish had taught. He'd argued that a smaller school might better meet Noah's needs, but Maggie and Noah had overruled him. Noah had taken the predictable path of wandering from major to major over his first year and a half. Once confronted with the need to declare a field of study, he'd announced fine art to be his choice and painting his concentration. The boy had talent, McTavish acknowledged to Maggie, but he wondered if Noah had the inner drive necessary to excel. Maggie acknowledged that she wasn't sure, but added, "Don't people make their real decisions in grad school these days?" Maybe, McTavish had thought, but an art degree didn't open up huge graduate school possibilities.

"Have you been able to get the classes you want?" McTavish asked, hoping for an easy entry to a conversation that had not always gone smoothly in the past.

"Mostly. I really wanted to get in a life painting class with Professor Inish this semester, but it filled with seniors, so I'll try again in the spring. I love my mixed media and basic color classes, but my drawing class is a drag."

Given his decision to forgo color until he felt more confident in his ability to draw, McTavish asked what the issue was.

"It's the instructor. All he does is bitch. He's an abstract painter who got assigned the class at the last minute and I guess he thinks it's beneath him."

"Drawing is beneath him?" McTavish asked.

"Yeah. He says that painting and color are the only things that matter. He keeps saying that 'Drawing is like the ABCs to a writer. They're important, they're the basics, but it's words that really matter and in art it's painting and color that matter.'"

"It's an interesting idea, but I'm not sure that the metaphor is accurate. Wouldn't it be more appropriate to think of words as the basics to a writer and the narrative as the equivalent of a painting?"

"I don't know. The guy is kind of a blowhard, but I agree with him. I know that you're all into drawing, Dad, but I've seen some of your paintings. They're not bad. I don't think you need to spend your time drawing. The real work is in the painting."

"Maybe so, son, but in time. Not now."

"Jesus, you're so stubborn. You always have to do things your own way." Pausing, Noah looked directly at his father. "Mom was right about you."

McTavish, trying to understand his son's sudden anger, said, "Your mom was right about a lot of things, but what in particular?"

"She said you'd always do things your own way. Didn't matter what anyone else thought or said or did. You had to do it your way. She'd say, 'Love him or hate him, your father will always be the man he is.' I never really understood what that meant until now. I think she meant you'd always be strong and stalwart and committed to doing good. And maybe all that's true, Dad, but I see you as cold and selfish and uncompromising. You say that you love me, but do you really? Can you really love anyone?" Noah threw down his silverware and stared at his father.

"I love you, Noah," McTavish said quietly, feeling an unnatural calm. "I love *you*." He got up from the table, picked up his dishes, took them to the sink, and began filling the dish pan with water.

Chapter 28

Given its limited publication schedule, only rarely did weekly newspapers like the *Rascal Harbor Gazette* score a scoop. Townsfolk loved the *Gazette*, but were used to reading reports of events well past their occurrence. This time, however, District Attorney Turcotte's decision to abandon the charges against James Park occurred in just enough time for Sarah McAdams to write the story and get it into the paper the same day as the state newspapers carried it. Stories in the latter were brief, a couple of paragraphs each in the Bangor and Portland papers. Sensing a coup, Nellie pushed Sarah to expand the story and gave it front page prominence.

McTavish awoke to his cell phone and a headache. The night before, Noah had joined him in washing the dinner dishes, but neither had spoken. Once finished, Noah had gone upstairs and McTavish did not seen him the rest of the evening. The Bushmills bottle did, however, and he'd not stopped when he should have.

The headache throb gained strength as Gary's voice boomed, "John, John! Jesus, did I wake you up? You don't sound so good."

McTavish wasn't sure how Gary could tell how his voice sounded as, as far as he knew, he'd only croaked out a "Hello."

Without pause, Gary pushed on. "It's done, John, it's done. Jimmy's free."

"He's free?" McTavish repeated in a voice he wasn't sure was his own.

"Yup, they dropped the charges and now he's free. It took 'em goddamned long enough, but he's free. We got the call from Julian late yesterday. It's in all the papers today."

McTavish could hear Ruby in the background, talking non-stop about a "Potty for Dimmy." He didn't have to ask as Gary hurtled on.

"Jesus, Ruby, hush up and I'll tell him," Gary said, with a hand over the receiver. Returning to McTavish, he said, "So we're havin' a party, John, and we want you and Noah to come. Tonight at 7. Ruby says you gotta come. She says if you don't come, she's gonna be 'mad as a drowned chicken!' I think she means a wet hen, but…well anyway, see ya tonight."

McTavish put down his phone, held his head in his hands, and wondered which had contributed more to the hammering he felt—Gary's torrent of words or his three.

Never one to lay abed, McTavish hoped to resolve his hangover with work. So he washed up, dressed, and made a pancake and bacon breakfast. Noah showed no signs of coming down so, after he ate, McTavish wrapped up Noah's breakfast for reheating later.

McTavish had been at his drawing table for an hour when Noah clomped down the stairs. The drawing he worked on featured a hand pointing an index finger. Noah poured himself a cup of coffee and slumped into a recliner. McTavish looked up and said, "I'm driving over to town to pick up the newspaper and a few art supplies. Would you like to come along?"

"Yes, I would. Thank you," Noah said formally.

"Later on, we've been invited to a party. Jimmy Park has been cleared of the theft and his family wants to celebrate."

"Okay," said Noah into his cup.

In silence, father and son readied themselves for the short trip to town. On the drive over, they decided that Noah would wander around the shops and galleries while McTavish did his shopping. Noah planned to walk back to the cottage in time for lunch. We're talking, McTavish thought to himself, sort of.

McTavish picked up the *Gazette*, but did little more than note the headline **Park Cleared of Theft** and think to himself, finally. He picked up his supplies, drove back to the cottage, and was working on his drawing when Noah arrived at noon.

Noah had overheard townsfolk discussing the news and so picked up the weekly from the dining room table. As McTavish made sandwiches for lunch, Noah read the account aloud:

In a release to the press, District Attorney Lee Turcotte announced on Tuesday that all charges were being dropped against Rascal Harbor resident James Park around the theft of the recently discovered Winslow Homer watercolor.

The release read, "After a thorough investigation, Chief Miles and I have concluded that insufficient evidence exists to proceed with an indictment against James Park. Consequently he is released of all charges. That said, should new evidence emerge, Mr. Park could be re-arrested and a probable cause hearing scheduled. A grand jury will be called soon to establish if probable cause exists to bring Simon Britton to trial."

Turcotte could not be reached for comment. In a telephone interview, Chief Miles refused to fully exonerate Park saying, "We don't have the evidence, but that doesn't mean Jimmy Park's not involved somehow. We're going to keep looking." Asked if he thought there was sufficient evidence to convict Simon Britton, Chief Miles said, "Absolutely," but refused to elaborate. Chief Miles added, however, that he believed Britton's trial would begin soon.

News of the announcement has spread quickly through town. Most of those interviewed reacted much as did Trudy Turner, owner of Lydia's Restaurant, who said, "About time. I don't think there were half a dozen people in town who believed Jimmy Park was guilty of anything." Robertay Harding, president of the Rascal Harbor Art Colony, agreed adding, "Seems like all the evidence is pointing toward Simon Britton. The man deserves a fair trial, but I would have to say that he looks guilty."

Some speculation continues, however, that Park and Britton conspired to commit the theft. Local resident Caleb Rimes said, "I think they was both involved. I ain't going to say any more than that."

Detective Richard Chambers said that the department had investigated the possibility of collusion and had failed to establish a credible link. "We now believe that Simon Britton acted alone and believe the evidence will clearly show that result," he said.

The rest of the story detailed the likelihood of calling a grand jury to establish whether sufficient cause existed to take the case to trial. As he finished reading, Noah looked up and said, "Well, that's good news for your friend and reason enough to have a party."

"It is. It's been tough on Jimmy and his family." McTavish paused and asked, "So do you want to go?"

"Sure. I want to meet these characters. You've described them pretty well, but I want to see for myself."

McTavish smiled. As he brought the food to the table, he asked, "Any obituaries?"

"Obituaries? Why?"

"If there are any, you'll see."

Noah thumbed through the paper to the right section. Silently scanning the first one, his eyes widened. "Jesus, Dad, what is this?"

"Hard to tell. Read it to me."

Noah read:

Randy Dickens, age 53, died Monday morning after landing on his head. Randy fell 25 feet off the staging he had erected for a siding job on Mary Merry's house at 69 Simmons Road. Aptly named, Randy was a popular fellow with the ladies of the Harbor. Also known as a good carpenter, Randy had no trouble finding places to drill, pound, and poke wood into any hole he could find. With no family to speak of, Randy's friends will hold a rally and collect money for the Rascal Harbor Ladies Auxiliary, to whom Randy made many donations in the past.

Finishing the piece, Noah said, "Jesus, that's practically pornographic. Who writes this stuff?"

"That would be Nellie Hildreth, the owner and editor of the paper. She has a unique way of representing the lives of the dead."

"Wonder what she'll write about you."

❧

The McTavishes passed the rest of the day industriously. McTavish worked on his drawing while Noah searched the Internet for images to include in a presentation he would make in his graphics class next week. Though they worked in the same room, neither spoke. Still, the tension evident last evening had evaporated. When he noticed, McTavish thought, gone, but not really gone…Christ, I sound like Maggie.

Chapter 29

McTavish and Noah arrived at the Parks' house to see the party in full blow. Some of Gary's friends decided that seven PM was far too late to start drinking so they'd arrived up at four. That they arrived with cases of beer made them quite welcome in Gary's eyes, though Ruby grumbled, "Dey here early so dey can eat up all my damn good food."

And it was good food, or what remained of it. McTavish and Noah picked through the left-overs as they picked their way through the crowd. Managing a plate and beer while elbows and hips bumped him, McTavish's food slid to the floor when Gary bear hugged him from behind. "John McTavish," Gary slurred into McTavish's ear. "Glad you could make it. Let's get a drink!"

McTavish thought he should introduce Noah around, but Gary had hold of his elbow and was steering him toward the living room where card tables were covered with beer and liquor. As they pushed forward, McTavish saw Louise Park approach Noah.

At the booze tables, Gary insisted on getting McTavish a beer despite the one already in his hand. McTavish relented, took the second beer, and discretely put the first down on a side table. "Jesus, John, I'm glad you're here."

"Oh?"

"You were there at the beginning. You were there when I got that first call from Jimmy. You kept me sane. It was you kept me sane."

McTavish didn't remember doing anything aside from listening, but Gary had already moved on.

"You are a wise man, Professker," Gary said, now leaning on McTavish's arm for support. "Me? I'm just a worried old dad. I want the best for the boy. I really do…I do…but, Jesus, he's got a tough road ahead. I mean, it's good he's off. It's really good. But Jesus…" Gary trailed off, but continued to stare deeply into McTavish's eyes. "You know what I'm saying, don't you." This last bit was phrased as a question, but came out a declaration. "Can you help him, John? You know, with the art stuff to be sure but, you know, with the other thing, too. Can you help him?" Gary still stared at McTavish, but his eyes had softened and his voice was pleading. "I do love that boy, John, but I'm worried. A dad gets worried. Maybe you could talk with him? Maybe just talk with him." Gary patted McTavish's arm, nodded to him in sober fashion, and pushed off to greet another guest.

"Don't even start," McTavish heard himself saying as Maggie's face loomed in his mind's eye. He knew she'd delight in the irony that he was being cast as savior to one boy when he had such trouble with him own. I'm going to need something more than beer, he thought, as he reached for the nearest bottle of brown liquor.

※

"Finally, we can move on," Robertay Harding said to a small group of local artists Jimmy had insisted be invited. "Our nightmare is almost over."

Though all nodded, Thomas Beatty said mildly, "Well, yes, Robertay, Jimmy's dilemma is resolved, but remember Simon's is still in process."

The group nodded at this point as well, but Robertay cut it short. "James Park has talent, Thomas. Talent! To think of that talent being locked away, well it's just insane. Now don't get me wrong. Simon's a good man, he's been a good friend to the Colony. But please don't confuse that friendship with talent. He dabbles, Thomas, he dabbles!"

"Ah, I suppose he does at that," Thomas said and the group nodded.

❀

"He's a fuckin' idjit," Minerva Williams said a bit too loudly. "Anyone who knows Caleb Rimes and has somethin' more than a brick for a brain knows that Caleb is a fuckin' idjit!" Caleb's speculations in the *Gazette* story and in shops around town were earning him few kudos.

"He may not be a *"fuckin'* idiot, but he is an idiot," added Maude Anderson.

Karen Tompkins said, "Idiot, fucking idiot, big fucking idiot, it really doesn't matter. The guy's a jackass of the first order and—"

"Hmmm. Let me see if I've got this right," Geraldine Smythe said. "Caleb is an idiot, a…"

The girls erupted in laughter.

❀

Jumper Wilson sported a new T-shirt for the party: *Better safe than sorry, but better sorry than in jail.*

❀

Noah was enjoying his time with Louise Park. He judged her to be about his age, but more importantly, he judged her to be much different than he expected the standard Rascal Harbor, twenty-something female to be. Noah had not spent much time in the Harbor growing up. His parents had been coming for 15 seasons or more, but he'd typically gone to summer camps in the Midwest and around the country.

Consequently he'd never really known any Harbor kids his age.

It was Louise who intercepted him. "You must be John's kid," she said, approaching with a beer in an outstretched hand. "You look just like him."

"I do?" Noah asked. He'd heard this comment before but, as he thought he favored his mother, it always surprised him.

"Well, yeah. I mean you've got the same hair and jawline, but it's mostly your eyes. You've got his eyes."

Noah expected he'd consider this line of thought later. For now he focused on the girl's own eyes, which had a dancing quality to them, and on her full-lipped smile, which stirred him. But instead of highlighting these attributes, Noah said, "And you've got your father's hands."

As they both looked in that direction, Noah silently kicked himself. Moron, he thought. For her part, Louise laughed.

Holding up her left hand, which had a small grease smudge on the side, she said, "Damn, guess I didn't clean up too well after leaving the garage. Nice of you to notice, though." She finished with another of those great smiles.

"I'm a moron."

"Yup, but at least you're not a 'fuckin' idjit.'" They both laughed, smiled, and drank.

※

More smiles ensued when Ruby approached Jimmy and the sculptor Jona Lewis. They had been debating the pros and cons of paint versus marble as a means of capturing human souls. Ruby, mug of Manischewitz in hand, said, "Boys, der is nothing like dem boots by Beans for soles. You can almost practically climb up a mountain in them." Then, looking around the room, she said, "Jesus, ain't that Jumper Wilson an oddball kind of a duck!"

GEOFFREY SCOTT

❦

Julian Pratt, who nobody liked to talk to, but everybody did, found himself surrounded by fans.

"You did Jimmy a good turn," Rob Pownall said. "I wondered if you'd be able to get him off the cops' radar." Ray Manley, Bill Candlewith, and Slow Johnston nodded in agreement.

"Aye. You did indeed," said Ray. "I kinda thought, once they got onto Simon, that they'd lock 'em both up in the same cell. Them being, well, y'know…"

"Artists?" Slow Johnston asked.

As everyone turned to Slow, Julian said, "Yes, Slow, they're both… artists." All but Slow chuckled. Slow smiled as though he'd solved the Great Train Robbery.

"I really didn't do all that much," Julian started to say in a rare moment of honesty. "I just—"

"You did what you needed to do," Rob said. "The boy needed a steady hand, someone who would stand up to the cops, especially that goddamned chief. And you did it."

"Well, really, gentlemen, the case was—" Julian tried again, but the men would have nothing of it.

"We suspect the boy's a little light in the loafers and we know that Simon's feet practically don't even touch the ground," Bill said. "But what's right's, right. And if the boy is innocent then he and his family ought not to be shamed."

Again, the men nodded gravely and, with that, Julian smiled and accepted their praise. To hell with the truth, he thought, it's highly overrated.

❦

Having recovered from his gaffe—or having Louise allow him to recover—Noah enjoyed talking with Louise. The girl had a lively brain, a quick laugh, and an ironic streak as wide as his own. They talked about art and cars and dreams. They also talked about McTavish.

"You're more like him than just in looks," Louise said. "You've got that same thing."

"'Same thing'?"

"Yup. You've got that smart, quiet confidence thing that's he's got. He's got more, but you've got a lot. Neither of you thinks you've to jabber on and on to impress people. You're more likely to ask a question and actually listen to what a person has to say. That's pretty cool."

Noah had heard that he looked something like his father; he'd not realized that he might also be like him in manner.

"And Jimmy just adores him," Louise continued. "He thinks your dad is the smartest artist he's met. Jimmy thinks most of the other artists in town are just posers. He says your dad hasn't had all the experience most of the local hacks do, but he's the real thing. He's smart about art, for sure, but Jimmy says he also feels it."

As Noah absorbed this view of his father, Bradley Little sidled over. Louise introduced them saying, "Noah's dad is the one Jimmy loves so much."

Bradley said, "Yeah, I know. They get along thick as thieves. But, you know, it's just art."

Louise stiffened. "Noah's an artist too, Bradley…and don't dismiss things you don't understand."

Bradley bristled a bit. Turning first to Noah, he grumbled, "Sorry, man." Then turning to Louise, he said, "What do you know about art? You're all into cars and shit."

Louise bristled in return. "There's art in everything, Bradley, even in your basketball playing. That's why I always liked to watch you. It was like you had this inner sense of what the game was all about and you got upset when your teammates couldn't see it."

Noah added, "Louise is right. Art isn't just about drawing or sculpting. It's about the *way* you do stuff, you know, trying to see below the surface of the everyday. Seeing what's really there, and then bringing out the stuff that's beautiful and right."

"Sounds a little la-di-dah to me," Bradley said.

"La-di-dah? Jesus, Bradley!" Louise said. "How can you have been friends with Jimmy all these years? You know how important art is to him."

"We get along, you know," Bradley said grumpily. "There's more to friends than what's on the surface."

"Exactly," Louise said delightedly. "I think that's just what Noah is trying to say. Art is the beauty below the surface—the beautiful break-away lay-up, the beautiful compression ratio in a '67 Mustang, the beautiful smile on the *Mona Lisa*."

Damn, she's a philosopher-mechanic! Noah thought as he tried to avoid staring puppy-eyed at Louise.

"Well, maybe," Bradley said, and huffed off.

"I really don't understand how those two have been friends so long," Louise said.

"Must be truly something deep, something Bradley can't even see."

Chapter 30

The celebration at the Parks' house went on for hours. The booze lasted long after the food did and the attendees apparently decided that the former would suffice. McTavish and Noah stayed until midnight, driving home slowly so as not to flag a policeman's attention. Anticipating his second hangover in as many days, McTavish loaded up on aspirin and prevailed on Noah to do the same before going to bed. Both expected to make a return trip to *that* bottle in the morning.

And they did. Bleary-eyed, they arrived in the kitchen at the same time the next morning. Each took a fistful of aspirin, and then stood in front of the coffee pot, hopeful that it had magically filled itself. After checking to be sure it hadn't, McTavish croaked, "Let's go to Lydia's."

Again driving slowly, though this time because every pothole bounce thundered through their heads, the McTavishes inched toward the diner. Parking the car, McTavish realized that this destination might be a mistake as the usual thrum of conversation at Lydia's was likely to send his headache into overdrive. The pull of hot coffee, however, proved powerful and so he and Noah climbed the steps and walked inside.

There they found a blissful quiet. Most of the patrons had spent time at Gary and Ruby's last night and so nursed their own throbbing heads. Trudy and Julia, sensing their customers' need for quiet, moved about, took orders, and delivered food like ghosts.

McTavish and Noah took seats at the counter and began their coffee cure when Caleb Rimes slammed through the door.

"Greetings happy residents of Rascal Harbor!" he said in a booming voice. Looking around the room, he continued, "Jesus Christ, what is this, a goddamned morgue? What's the matter, you wimps can't hold your liquor?" Laughing loudly, he asked, "How are those heads today? Anybody want a beer? A shot of whiskey? No?" As Caleb walked through the room, he slapped men on the back, winked at women, and hailed most everyone but McTavish and Noah by name.

"Stow it, Caleb," Trudy said with an edge in her voice. "No one needs to listen your yap this morning."

"Ah, Trudy, you know you've missed me," Caleb replied with as much sweetness as he could manage. Looking at the patrons, he said, "Just trying to spread a little good cheer."

"Well cheer your ass right out of here if you can't keep it down," Trudy replied. Caleb smiled a shit-eater's grin and continued to the men's table at the rear.

As he approached, Minerva said, just loud enough for both tables to hear, "I smell a fart, a great big ripper of a fart…anyone else smell a great big ripper of a fart?" Quiet laughter echoed around both tables.

"Oh fu…oh forget you, Minerva, you dried up old flounder," Caleb said, biting back his anger. "Wonder you can smell anything at all after dishing up that slop at the cafeteria all those years."

"Ah, the prodigal jackass returns," Rob Pownall said. "Sit down, Caleb, and shut up."

Caleb smiled at the ladies, turned to the men's table, and slid into a chair next to Slow Johnston who gave him an uncertain smile. "Back and better than ever," Caleb said, though a bit quieter than before.

"Doubt that," Vance Edwards said, then turned back to Bill Candlewith and Rob and continued with the conversation about the Red Sox's chances of landing a hot free agent pitcher.

"What was that all about?" Noah asked his father.

"Small town personalities with oversized mouths," McTavish said.

"Louise says you and I have the same mouth. Well, not the same mouth, but the same jawline. And she says we talk, or don't talk, the same way."

"Noah, if I didn't have a headache, you might be talking sensibly, but I do and you aren't," McTavish said slowly as each word reverberated through his skull.

"I know. It made sense at the time." Noah paused, took another sip of coffee. "I guess she was saying that we might be more alike that it appears."

"Ah, I suppose that strikes you as a cross to bear," said McTavish gently.

Noah's eyes flashed, but he said only, "Yes and no."

Full of donuts and coffee, the McTavishes drove back to the cottage. Once there, McTavish decided to stack wood rather than go to his drawing table. He'd had a couple cords of green oak and maple delivered a year ago. Now dry and prime for the wood stove, he'd begun stacking it in four by eight foot tiers. He was surprised, and pleased, when Noah found a pair of gloves and started helping him. They worked silently for an hour until each had a light sweat going.

"Expect we've burned most of the alcohol off by now," McTavish said. Heading for the cottage, he asked, "Ready for another cup of coffee?"

"I am," Noah said and followed his father into the kitchen.

Both men worked on their respective projects for the rest of the day. They talked in passing and at lunch, but only about things innocent and inconsequential.

GEOFFREY SCOTT

Late in the day, McTavish walked by Noah who was working on his laptop at the kitchen table. "Is that your graphics project?"

Still looking at his screen, Noah said, "Yeah. My professor is a nut about negative space. He says it's just as important as the actual objects in an image. I hadn't thought about it much before, but I'm beginning to think he's right. It's pretty cool to think that you can create images by what you don't put in as well as what you do."

"I see you went with Rubin's classic face-vase image for one of your pieces. People call it an optical illusion, but I think that's being dismissive. Makes it sound like the image is just a trick."

"I think I agree with you. It's a pretty stark example of positive and negative space, but it's the same concept that Escher and every other artist uses. My professor says that the Japanese even have a word for it—*ma*. It means the gap or space around an object, a kind of form and unform."

"And every donut maker knows the same thing," McTavish mused. Seeing his son's confused look, McTavish waved off his own comment, saying, "Just something I've been thinking about."

Noah put the shine on his project, and then readied himself for an evening out with Louise Park. McTavish seated himself at his drawing table for the first time that day.

An hour or so after Noah left, McTavish heard a knock on his kitchen door and Jimmy Park call out, "Hello, John." McTavish had heard a car drive up and suspected it was Jimmy from the distinctive rattle of a heat shield that had come loose and stayed that way.

Greeting his visitor in the kitchen, McTavish realized that he, Noah, and most of Lydia's diners were not the only ones to have suffered from the previous night's event. Jimmy still looked a bit unsteady. "Got a little too far into your cups last night, James?" McTavish asked.

"Not sure what that means, but if it means being sloshed or 'three shits to the wind' as my mother says, then yes."

STEALING HOMER

McTavish chuckled. "So how does it feel to be a free man?"

"Pretty good, but I won't lie—the thought that the police might still try to come after me is a little scary. People keep telling dad that Chief Miles has got it out for me."

"I've heard that too, but it sounds like they're focused on Simon now, otherwise I don't think they'd have dropped the charges against you."

"I hope you're right," Jimmy said. "I still hate to think that Simon was the thief and I really hate the idea that he framed me, but if he did…"

"Well, I suppose we'll see soon."

"Soon, but not soon enough."

The two men spent the rest of the evening talking about negative and positive space and arguing, largely for the sake of argument, about which was more important. When Noah returned from his date with Louise, he listened for a long time before entering the conversation. McTavish tried to draw him in at various times and that effort sometimes worked. Still, Noah seemed distant and distracted, his contributions to the discussion desultory at best. Eventually, he excused himself and went off to bed. McTavish and Jimmy continued their chat, McTavish putting Noah's behavior down as an after-effect of the date with Louise.

CHAPTER 31

The next morning McTavish awoke glad to be hangover free. He made coffee and settled into a kitchen rocker while Noah slept in. Knowing that he would be taking Noah back to the airport later in the morning, McTavish reminisced as he rocked.

Noah had been precocious from birth, advancing quickly on both intellectual and physical fronts. He spoke and read and drew earlier than the kids around him; he grew taller and rolled over and walked earlier, too. Noah was a quiet, self-engaging kid who was equally content by himself or with others around. His generally earnest countenance melted, however, when he smiled. Yet that smile failed to mask the tinge of melancholy McTavish always sensed in his son. Maggie's smile, McTavish now thought, my melancholy.

As McTavish's memories bounced around, he realized that the cottage bore little evidence of Noah. A few of the boy's early drawings were tacked to the walls, but wherever McTavish looked, he saw only things that he and Maggie had contributed. Maybe the reason Noah took so much time looking around the cottage that first day, McTavish now realized, was that he was looking for traces of himself.

McTavish knew why Noah's presence was so absent in the cottage: The boy had spent very little time there. He and Maggie had bought the fixer-upper ten years ago. Noah, eleven years old at the time, had come with them that first summer and had seemed to enjoy himself. But succeeding summers found Noah off to one summer camp after another as Maggie and McTavish tried to support his meandering interests. Stamp camp, tennis camp, music camp—Noah had tried them all. He'd liked them all, too, but once each was done, he was on to something else. Meanwhile, he missed the life McTavish envisioned for him in Rascal Harbor. McTavish had even put his foot down when Maggie told him that Noah wanted to go to "reading camp" during his sixteenth summer. "Christ, can't he read in Rascal Harbor?" he had asked. Noah ended up going to a botany camp instead.

Noah's connection to the Rascal Harbor cottage, then, had been through his father and his mother, and now his mother was gone. At various points over the last few days, McTavish had mused that this might be the first of many times he and Noah would spend together at the cottage. At the same time, he could not shake the thought that it might also be one of the last.

That thought grew stronger on the drive to the airport.

The day started without incident. McTavish's emergent worry faded as Noah woke late, ate a hearty breakfast, and efficiently packed his gear. McTavish hoped that this seemingly tranquil mood reflected a softening of their relationship, though he suspected it was largely due to a lovely evening with Louise Park.

Noah responded vaguely to McTavish's gentle questions about the evening. "She's a nice girl," he had said eventually. "Turns out we have some common interests." Pressed for details, Noah said, "Well, art and music and politics. Louise says she's like one of three liberals in the whole town. Said it drives her father crazy."

Knowing Gary Park's aversion to all things regulatory, McTavish expected that Louise's views ran at hard right angles to her father's. Ruby, by contrast, was fiercely independent of mind, choosing candidates for reasons that often seemed unfathomable. McTavish had once heard Ruby extoll a local candidate's hands. "Dat Ralph Richards, he got dem big muscle hands. I bet he make a damn good select person guy."

Though curious about whether Louise had made any more comparisons between himself and Noah, McTavish decided to let the question lie. He helped Noah load his bags into the Saab and they headed to Portland.

As McTavish drove, however, Noah seemed to grow agitated. Initially, he appeared contemplative, quietly watching the landscape roll by. He adjusted his seat a couple of times, finally complaining that the Saab's old seat "Would break the back of a normal person."

Seeming resigned to his discomfort, Noah rolled his passenger-side window up and down a couple of times and fiddled with the radio. Eventually McTavish asked, "Something gnawing at you?"

Noah ignored the question, harrumphing back in his seat. When McTavish persisted, asking, "What's upsetting you?"

"Jesus, Dad, you just don't get it, do you?"

Taken aback, McTavish asked, "What don't I get?"

"Do you care about me at all?" Noah asked, fire in his accusation. Without waiting for an answer, he continued, "Do you even know anything about me? I mean, what is it about Jimmy Park that's so fascinating? Do you know that you can't go fifteen minutes without talking about him or talking to him? Jesus, Dad, is he like the son you never had?"

"Where is all this coming from, Noah?" McTavish asked, completely at sea now.

"It's obvious isn't it?"

"No, it's not obvious. I don't know what you're talking about." McTavish was trying hard to be patient.

"Louise told me that Jimmy is like over the moon about you, that he thinks you're some kind of god," Noah said, his voice quavering. "Jesus, Dad, don't you know how much that hurts me? Do you really like him that much more than me? Is he the artist son you always wanted?"

Before McTavish could answer, Noah continued, "I mean I saw you two last night. It's the most alive I've seen you since I got here." Taking a breath, Noah said quietly, "I know you tried to bring me into the conversation when I got back, but I felt like a third thumb. I can see how Jimmy feeds off you and you encourage him like you never did me. And so I just want to know—is he the son you always wanted?"

When McTavish didn't answer immediately, Noah turned directly toward him and demanded, "Well?"

McTavish had no words. Noah's anger seemed so deep and so irrational, McTavish could not figure out where to begin. Even if he had had words to comfort and reassure his son, McTavish was not sure he could have gotten them out.

His silence damned him. "Just as I thought…'silent presence,'" Noah said shaking his head. "A goddamned silent presence."

CHAPTER 32

This last exchange occurred as the Portland airport came into view. McTavish navigated to the departure gates entrance in silence as his son's accusations reverberated throughout his brain. Words and half thoughts tumbled around inside, but nothing came out. When he pulled into a parking spot, Noah looked at him again, closed his eyes, and shook his head.

"Don't bother to turn off the car," Noah said. "I'll just get my stuff out of the trunk."

"I can help you," McTavish said, finally able to express a coherent thought.

"No thanks, Dad, you've done enough."

And then he was gone. McTavish watched Noah walk rapidly toward the terminal, backpack swaying but without a look backward. McTavish thought he saw Noah's head turn as he opened the door, but he couldn't be sure.

After a couple of minutes, McTavish started the car. Before shifting it into gear, however, he turned off the key, pounded his fist on the steering wheel, and shouted, "Goddamn you, Maggie! Goddamn you, goddamn you! Why did you leave me when you knew I didn't know what I'm doing? I don't know what I'm doing, Maggie! Goddamn it, why did you have to die?"

And then the tears came. The tears that hadn't come when Maggie told him about the cancer, the tears that hadn't come when he sat at Maggie's bedside, the tears that hadn't come at Maggie's funeral. McTavish leaned his head against the steering wheel and cried, silently at first, and then in wracking sobs. And all he could think was, I'm broken, Maggie, I'm broken. You kept me glued together, but I'm broken. I know I can't fix you. I know I can't fix Noah. But mostly I know that I can't fix myself, Maggie, because I don't even know what I am without you.

At this thought, McTavish sat back and rubbed the tears from his eyes. I don't even know what I am without her, he thought, repeating the line over and over in his head.

And then he thought, but Christ I have to be something…something apart from Maggie. She's gone, that piece of me that was with her is gone and I'm not going to get it back.

It was then that McTavish realized that Maggie had not spoken to him once since Noah's departure. He'd heard no voice in his head, not one of her gentle, prodding, loving, scolding words. Maggie's voice was silent.

"Jesus, Maggie, now you go quiet?" he said aloud, still staring out the windshield at the airport door Noah had entered, "Now you have nothing to say?"

McTavish knew that Maggie's silence had to mean something, she had to be pushing him toward some deeper insight. But he was damned if he could figure it out. Aloud, he said, "What am I supposed to be, Mags, without you? Well, according to my son, I'm a shitty father and, according to my wastepaper basket, I'm a shitty artist. I thought I was a pretty good teacher at one point, but maybe I was shitty at that, too."

And at that moment he heard Maggie, or maybe he heard himself, or perhaps he heard generations of hardscrabble Mainers. The source suddenly mattered less than the message—"John Louis McTavish, stop whining, stop feeling sorry for yourself, and stop fussing about. Get your ass in gear."

As McTavish took this in, he had to chuckle. Jesus, he thought, this is my epiphany? "Get your ass in gear?" That's it? McTavish started the car, but before he pulled away, he thought, maybe I'll get a bumper sticker…

McTavish had not even left the airport grounds when he realized that the bumper sticker comment was one of his standard responses to dealing with a stressful situation. Humor had saved him many times in the past. Maybe not with Noah, but it had with Maggie, his colleagues, his relatives. And himself, he now acknowledged. A bit of humor eased the anxiety, gave him some breathing space, and allowed him to escape. It was a bullshit move he knew. It lightened a situation and Maggie had accepted it. But she'd also made it clear she knew his humor was a dodge. The thing is, it worked, or it seemed to. He now knew that it really didn't. You're an idiot, McTavish, he said to himself before Maggie could.

His brain tumbled as McTavish drove home. Once again, he found it impossible to hold a coherent line of thought, to work through just one of the many messes he now could not avoid. "A silent presence" his son had said of him. If only Noah could see my brain now, McTavish thought, it's far from silent up there.

McTavish's brain continued to burble as he drove up to his cottage. Getting out of the car, he hesitated before going in as if putting off a visit to the dentist. Instead, he wandered his small piece of property, picking up fallen limbs, and kicking his feet through the accumulating leaves. Pointless, he thought, and so decided that work might prove a balm. Yet, even stacking wood failed to calm the tumult in his thoughts. Though he expected no relief, McTavish put away his work gloves and went into his cottage. He laid down on his couch and looked for answers in the rafters. Within minutes, he was sound asleep.

McTavish awoke with a start two hours later. He could not recall dreaming or experiencing any flashes of insight, but his brain and body both felt calmed. Am I dead? he wondered. How would I know if I was? He pondered these questions until he realized that he must have fallen asleep on his right hand for it now felt like it was full of bees. Dead people's arms don't buzz, he reasoned, guess I'm still alive. So he got up, stretched, and sat down at his drawing table. He didn't know what had settled his brain during the nap, but he was content to let it be for now.

CHAPTER 33

Simon Britton had waived his right to a grand jury, opting instead for a preliminary hearing. Doing so tickled Rascal Harbor residents: Grand juries are closed; probable cause hearings are open to the public. The latter typically last only a couple of hours at the most, but the idea of witnessing the event fluttered the hearts of many townsfolk.

The high estimated value of the Homer painting made its theft a Class B crime and so pushed it into the Superior Court realm. Judge Langston was a Rascal Harbor native, but his courtroom was in Herrington, the county seat.

Herrington and Rascal Harbor were rivals of sorts. No one alive could remember the origin of the rivalry and it mostly applied to local sports teams. Still Rascal Harbor residents disliked the idea of "Traipsing all the way upta Herrington" as Minerva Williams put it. The "traipse" was only ten miles, but physical distance is only one kind.

Of Lydia's back-table patrons, only Minerva, Geraldine Smythe, and Rob Pownall were able to make the trip. While Rob drove and Geraldine rode shotgun, Minerva sat in the back seat and played with her new Facebook account. Her daughter, Bev, had bought her a smartphone, set up the account, and sent out friend requests to all of Minerva's buddies. The training session to use the phone had taken nearly two hours, a six-pack of beer, and three major fights, but Minerva was now as tech-savvy as any seventy-year-old in Rascal Harbor. And over the short drive to Herrington, Minerva made three posts:

Heading to Herrington. Rob driving like a maniac.

Jesus, ain't the trees pretty this year.

Caleb Rimes is a dumbass.

Minerva intended to erase the last message before she sent it, but Rob hit a pothole and her typing finger hit the "post" button and the damn thing went live. She mumbled, "Ah well, ain't like it's gonna be news to anyone, includin' himself."

It took Rob three trips around the Herrington courthouse to find a place to park. He and the ladies cursed all the "nosy gawkers" who had the same intention they did, and beat them to all the good parking spots. Inside the courthouse, they managed to find three seats, though not together. Minerva immediately posted, "Half the people here ain't even from the Harbor. Don't these folks have nothing better to do?"

As the hearing advanced, Minerva's attention wandered. Ignoring the actual proceedings, her posts focused on the participants…and the crowd:

Christ, old Simon looks like he just crawled out of the grave.

That Paul Reny is a good looking man, for a Frenchman.

Look at that Chief Miles. The man makes toads look handsome.

Robertay Harding has got the biggest boobs I have ever seen!

Jesus, ain't that Paul Reny some handsome.

Just saw the ugliest woman on the planet. Must be a Herrington gal.

Simon ain't faring well. Looks like he might melt into his chair.

Saw Jumper—how the hell did he get up here? His shirt says,

'God helps those who help themselves to good lawyers.'

After this last post, Judge Langston presumably made his ruling for Minerva's next post reported, *He's done for. Simon's got himself indicted.* She followed that with, *Christ, I feel sorry for the poor bastard.*

Though Minerva's reporting left a little to be desired in terms of motions, arguments, and the like, she did manage to capture the essence: Whether the evidence presented by the state would convince a jury or not, it was enough for a probable cause determination. Simon Britton was indicted and his case would be going to trial. Worse, Simon was going back to jail.

Minerva's friends back in the Harbor knew the result immediately. Because of their reposting abilities, most everyone in town soon knew, as well. Folks had mixed feelings about Simon's culpability, but they now knew that his day of reckoning was at hand.

Chapter 34

Because he eschewed Facebook, McTavish got the news about Simon Britton's indictment the old-fashioned way—Gary told him.

McTavish had a front passenger-side tire that wouldn't stay inflated. Gary suspected a faulty valve stem so he'd told McTavish to bring his car in for a new one the morning after the preliminary hearing. As Gary put the Saab on the lift to remove the tire, he said, "Suppose you heard about Simon." He hadn't, so McTavish just shrugged. "They got him. Judge Langston indicted him, so he's going to trial."

"Guess the DA must have presented a good argument. Doesn't sound good for Simon."

"All they got is circum, circum-something evidence, no eyewitnesses or nothing, but I guess they could still put him away if the jury agrees."

"Can't imagine Simon doing all that well in Warren if they do."

"Nor can I, but goddamn him if he did do it and he tried to get Jimmy in trouble, too. I just can't abide that. No sir, that just ain't right. Still, Ruby heard he looks a fright. Guess Minerva's been all over the Face-thing with news about him and the hearin'. Said Simon looks like a pale ghost of himself."

"Hopefully the trial will sort it all through, and then we'll know what really happened." Though he sort of believed this, McTavish knew that trials did not always result in such clarity. They might define a verdict, but there was always more to a story as complicated as this one. He knew there would be a judgment; he was less sure it would answer all the questions.

Chapter 35

Simon Britton's indictment created rich fodder for far more conversations than that between Gary Park and John McTavish. A good number of those conversations centered on the hearing itself and the decision made. Were a survey done, however, the results would show an equally large number of discussions focused on Minerva Williams's Facebook postings. And of those discussions, most highlighted the notion that Facebook might not be the best medium for a crazy person.

❦

Minerva's posts occupied a lot of attention, but not all of it. At the Rascal Harbor police station, the talk was about the victory and the vindication Judge Langston had just handed them. Though they all knew that an indictment was only a single step down the road to a conviction, it was a big step to be sure. If history was any guide, an indicted person was a guilty person in Rascal Harbor. District Attorney Lee Turcotte had his scruples, but he also had an excellent conviction record. The Harbor police felt they had reason to celebrate.

Chief Lawton Miles reveled in the considerable attention accorded the indictment. While he smiled at everyone, he surveyed the lobby for those who might do him and his department the most good. Maneuvering his bulky frame around the crowded station posed a challenge, but the oiliness that appeared to surround the chief's success seemed to smooth his movements.

In a corner of the station, Rendall Kalin tried hard to maintain his central role in unraveling the crime. Ignoring the fact that he had significantly compromised the evidentiary value of the back door key, he told whomever would listen that it was "Just good solid police work" that underlay the discovery. Also ignoring the fact that he'd been sent back to the gallery as a punishment, Kalin said, "I just had that cop feeling that I'd find a clue. You know that cop sense, the one all good policemen share." Most of those who Kalin addressed just stared back at him and shook their heads. But the station was full of cop friends and family, so he had multiple opportunities to share his story.

By contrast, Detective Dick Chambers fended off all well-wishers and hunkered down in his office. He expected the indictment; in fact, he would have been shocked if Judge Langston had decided otherwise. Yet Chambers took no great joy in this resolution. For one, he wished there was more, and more substantial, evidence of Simon's involvement. The facts were clear and pointed clearly in Simon's direction. Still, Chambers knew that pointing was not the same thing as proving. Chambers's second discomfort came from seeing Simon Britton, the prisoner. He could not get over how wretched this once-proud man appeared. And if Simon could look this bad based on a couple weeks in a local jail, he couldn't imagine how Simon would look after a stretch in the state penitentiary in Warren.

Chambers's first police partner had been a bitter old hand who took it as his responsibility to ride the rookie into being a good cop or out of the force. "You're too fuckin' soft, Chambers," his partner said fifteen minutes into their first shift, and then seemingly every other day until he retired two years later. His parting comment then: "You're still too goddamned soft, Chambers. But you're also a good cop. Don't let the first get in the way of the second."

Recalling this advice, Chambers thought he had followed it in the Britton case. Still, it brought no peace.

✺

Congregating at the gallery, the Rascal Harbor Art Colony board talked quietly among themselves until Robertay Harding called the emergency meeting to order. Jona Lewis, Toni Ludlow, and Thomas Beatty took their customary seats, each looking quickly and covertly at the empty chair that Simon Britton typically occupied. "Yes, yes, I know, that's one of our first orders of business," Robertay's voice boomed, after noticing her colleagues' glances. "We'll need to recruit a new member of the board. I have a list of prospects and I've got my eye on one… oh, but I'm getting ahead of myself." Robertay stopped, shuffled some papers around, and continued. "You'll just have to excuse me, I've been unnerved by the hearing and the indictment and Simon."

Sensing an expression of genuine concern, Thomas said, "There, there, Robertay. Simon is on all of our minds. He's such a gentle—"

"Oh, for Christ's sake, Thomas, stop your fussing. Simon has gotten himself into the fix and is bringing the Colony down as well," Robertay said, snapping at him. "If you're going to sit around feeling sorry for Simon—if you're going to put his welfare above the Colony's—well, then you can just resign!"

Thomas replied soothingly, "Robertay, Robertay, I only meant that perhaps we might keep our dear colleague in our best thoughts."

"Best thoughts? Simon should have given his 'best thoughts' to the Colony and kept his hands off the Homer. He's brought shame on himself and scandal onto the Colony, and I won't have it! I just won't have it!"

Trying to ease the tightness in the room, Toni said calmly, "So do you have some thoughts, Robertay? About how we ought to proceed, that is."

With the group's eyes still on her, Robertay took Toni's cue, pulled herself up to her full seated height, and said, "I do, Toni. I certainly

GEOFFREY SCOTT

do." Passing around copies of an agenda, she said, "I believe we have two items to discuss. First is our response to Simon's indictment and second is how we will replace him and with who."

"With whom, and I believe that is three items in total," Thomas said quietly.

Busying her paperwork, Robertay did not hear Thomas's comments. Jona Lewis did, and he gave Thomas a quick nod.

Sending around copies of a single-printed page, Robertay said, "I've taken the liberty of drafting a response from the Board to this horrendous situation." As her colleagues read, Robertay continued. "I think it hits all the right notes without sounding defensive. It's authoritative without seeming insensitive, it's descriptive without being melodramatic, it's concise and thorough. I think it's sufficiently clear that we need not waste time discussing it now."

As intended, this last comment silenced any immediate attempt to wordsmith the draft. "I'll be happy to entertain your suggestions, if you send them to me in an email," Robertay said. "But please do be quick about it as I want to get the piece to the *Gazette* in time for the next issue. I think it most important that the Colony announce its perspective as soon as possible."

With the matter of a Board response addressed, but not debated, Robertay moved to the second item on her list. Here, she withdrew a few sheets poorly stapled together. Waving the document in the air, she said, "I've looked at our bylaws, and, of course, it offers useful guidance as to how we should proceed."

Licking her index finger, Robertay turned to the second page, made some reading noises, looked up at the group, and said, "Yes, yes, it's quite clear. So we, the Board, are to put together a list of prospective members, discuss the list, and vote. Whoever receives the most votes will join our cheery group." At the word "cheery," Toni and Jona looked at each other and grimaced.

Missing the board members' look, Robertay carried on. "Now I know that we have some stellar possibilities among the membership but, as you know, not everyone is capable of carrying the mantle of leadership. I humbly serve as your president, but I can only do so because of your individual and collective intelligence, drive, common sense, and dedication. Those are the qualities we must look for in our replacement for Simon."

"Has Simon resigned?" Jona asked, interrupting Robertay's solo.

Flustered and irritated by this intrusion, Robertay stumbled. "Well…well, of course, well, no he hasn't *formally* resigned, but—"

"Well then, isn't it premature to be trying to replace him?" Jona asked. "After all, Simon's been indicted, but he hasn't gone to trial and he certainly hasn't been convicted."

"Jona has a point," Toni said matter-of-factly.

Blustering as she tried to regain her bearings, Robertay said, "Well, of course, he has a point, but I'm sure Simon will see his way to resigning. I mean, it's the proper thing to do. We can't have a felon on the board…"

"But that's just it," Jona said. "He's not a felon at this point and I, for one, am not interested in forcing his hand. Simon's got enough to worry about without having it appear that his friends are abandoning him."

"Well! I will not be browbeaten by a board member who fails to see the gravity of our situation!" Robertay replied crossly.

"Jona is not browbeating you, Robertay," Thomas said quietly. "He's just trying to make the point."

"I know exactly what point Jona Lewis is trying to make!" Robertay shouted, her voice rising in tone and severity with each word. "He has no regard for the disaster that looms before us or for my leadership in this situation. I will restore this ship with or without his help!"

"This is bullshit," Jona said as he stood. "I'll read your draft and send you some comments, but I'm not going to help you push Simon out."

As Jona left the room, Robertay first fumed, then turned to the remainder of the group and announced, "This meeting is adjourned."

When Thomas seemed about to say that the chair cannot adjourn a meeting, he saw the fury flying across Robertay's face and held the thought.

※

At Lydia's Diner, the normal distribution of gender, class, and seating had completely broken down. Men and women talked in animated fashion, the unemployed mingled with the trust funders, and the back tables were abandoned as everyone stood, sat, leaned, and lounged in the main dining area. There were no shouts or loud exhortations, but the number of people talking and the constant level of chatter raised a din that annoyed Trudy and Julia. They took orders and placed them with the cook…and then had to search for their customers as no one seemed to be in the same seat as when the order was placed. "Jesus, this place is nuthouse," Trudy said to Julia in passing.

Julia winked and held up a fistful of tip money. "Yeah, but looks like crime does pay…for some of us."

Chapter 36

Of course, face-to-face conversations at Lydia's, in the supermarket, over coffee, and across a bait barrel were only some of the ways that Rascal Harbor residents expressed their ideas. Facebook, Instagram, Twitter, email, and mobile phones buzzed as well.

The *Gazette* solidified community sentiment. Sarah McAdams's report of the preliminary hearing highlighted the front page—along with a traffic accident on Route 17 and a school board meeting on the question of buying new uniforms for the girls' field hockey team. The regular letters to the editor section doubled in size and featured a piece by Robertay and the Art Colony board. The typical Harbor notes and news filled the rest of the paper. Nellie Hildreth, anticipating an increase in readership, ordered the printing of an extra 150 copies. She was wise to do so.

Despite her unfinished journalism degree, Sarah McAdams was a competent reporter. She offered no flash or clever phrasings. She anticipated her readers' interests and questions and she addressed them with clear and coherent prose. Nellie Hildreth printed Sarah's work with only the barest editorial touch.

Those who wrote letters to the editor, by contrast, paid only passing attention to clarity or coherence or commas. From rants to soliloquies and recitations to bluster, the space devoted to readers' opinions ran the gamut. Few *Gazette* readers expected to learn much of anything new, but they all delighted in seeing their neighbors' pronouncements.

Most of those pronouncements in the week's issue spoke of the hearing in Herrington and of the implications for life in the Harbor as the case ran on. A few letters spoke to other town business—the price of medical coverage for town employees, the state of the library repair budget, and the success of the high school chess team in a state-wide competition. A couple of out-of-state letter writers marveled at the beauty of the fall foliage. One called it a "symphony of shining shades" while another remarked that the various red, yellow, and orange hues inspired thoughts of "God's heavenly palette." Nellie left these rhetorical fancies as is, but she had to bite her blue editor's pencil to do so.

The biggest topic, of course, was the case against Simon Britton.

> *To the Editor: I certainly do not know if Simon Britton is guilty and nobody else in this town does either. But I'm awfully glad to see Jimmy Park cleared of the charges and I wish him well. Go Sox!*
>
> *Rodney Glazer*

> *To the Editor: The DA, that Lee Turcotte, made a mighty strong case against Simon Britton up to Herrington the other day. I was there! Sitting in the second row and I could see everything that Turcotte did and he convinced me and everyone sitting around me.*
>
> *Lenny Cliff*

> *To the Editor: The theft of the Winslow Homer painting is a stain on the Harbor's standing. Although I am not a member of the local artist guild, I can see the benefits of being known as an art-friendly community. That the painting was stolen from our town and probably by an artist sends very*

bad signals to the rest of the world. I hope we can recover our good name.

Jennifer Lyndon

To the Editor: I would like to personally thank Chief Miles and the wonderful men and women of the Rascal Harbor Police Department for their fine work in bringing the evidence to bear in the case of the stolen painting!!! I don't want to rush to a verdict (well, actually I do—this drama has gone on long enough!!!), but I am confident that when Simon Britton finally goes to trial for this robbery, it will be because of the many efforts of our police force!!! I hope the voters remember this fact when it comes time to vote on the police department budget next year!!!

Mae Parton

To the Editor: Simon Britton is pathetic. The Sox are pathetic. The fishing's pathetic. If it weren't for bad luck, we'd be having no luck at all.

Jerry Glenville

As these letters were read, analyzed, and discussed across the Harbor, residents alternatively smiled, shook their heads, and swore. They talked to themselves, their spouses, their friends, and their neighbors, and they did so in person, over the phone, through emails, and via social media. The buzz created by the theft—not the goddamn "robbery," Sarah McAdams thought—had ebbed and flowed since its discovery. Simon Britton's indictment and the town's reactions to it in the *Gazette* re-energized the flow.

That flow gathered even more energy when readers saw the Art Colony response to the preliminary hearing. More than a letter to the editor, but less than a news story, the piece Robertay crafted offered little in the way of new information about the case. It did, however, offer some insights into the Colony board thinking, all of which reinforced some local opinions about the group and created a whole raft of others.

> *To the Peaceful Residents of Rascal Harbor*
>
> *We, the undersigned members of the Rascal Harbor Art Colony board, believe that we owe the community our measured thoughts about the recent troubles that have beset our town in general and our organization in particular. To that end, we submit the following for the town's careful consideration.*
>
> *The RH Art Colony was founded in 1885 for the promotion of artists and art in all forms. Since that time, members have represented their ideas in graphic media, in stone, in papier mâché, in wood, and in metals. We have welcomed works in all the glorious formats in which humans conceive of and express their ideas. We have also welcomed artists of all genders, races, ethnicities, and persuasions. Art knows only the limits that art knows! From the beginning, we have created and maintained the kind of "big tent" that politicians so like to describe and yet so seldom achieve.*
>
> *Against this background, the recent incident involving the theft of a previously unknown Winslow Homer watercolor has struck the Colony to its core. For years, we have staged numerous events, big and small, simple and elaborate that celebrate the art works produced by our members and by visitors to our region. Each of these events has contributed in some fashion to raising the consciousness of our community and to the significant role art can and should play in developing and supporting the common good. These are no small offerings, but we extend them with glad hearts and our warmest intentions.*
>
> *To now face the possibility, even the probability, that*

one of our own violated the community's trust in general and the Colony's trust in particular cannot go unheeded. Please know, peaceful residents, that the Art Colony Board of Directors takes this matter most seriously. We have discussed it at length and we are devising a plan ready to implement at a moment's notice. It is our fondest hope that this plan will restore the good name and the good standing of this revered organization. To that aim, we pledge our every effort. We hope for your support; we ask for your prayers.

Simply and sincerely,
The Rascal Harbor Board of Directors
Robertay Harding, President

"What a self-serving pile of horseshit," Nellie said after her first reading. Robertay had delivered the piece to the newspaper building herself, sweeping into the main office as though she were conveying the last of the Ten Commandments.

"I have come with a missive from the Colony," Robertay said. "Of course, I wouldn't *ask* that you print it on the front page…but if it could be placed in a prominent position in the paper, I do believe it would be seen as a public service."

Rich Reed, the paper's managing editor, had received Robertay, had taken responsibility for her piece, and had thanked her while nudging her toward the door. He'd done all of this to keep Nellie from coming out of her office and confronting Robertay just for the sport of it. Rich wasn't sure what source lay behind the antagonism Nellie felt toward Robertay. For her part, Robertay appeared oblivious to Nellie's dislike—Rich suspected that Robertay might be oblivious to quite a few people's views of her—and seemed to think them the best of pals. Rich knew otherwise and so kept the peace by keeping the two women apart.

Without reading it, Rich delivered Robertay's manuscript to Nellie with the single comment, "Robertay thinks this piece ought to be prominently displayed in the next issue." Rich was almost back to his own office when he heard Nellie snort. Knowing that it was only the opening salvo, he turned back, walked into Nellie's office, and sat tentatively in one of her chairs.

"What a goddamned nerve that woman's got," Nellie said. "She waltzes in here with this piece of nonsense and expects it to be printed on the front page?"

"Well, she said she wouldn't *ask* for that placement, but I suspect it would please her," Rich said calmly.

"Pleasing Robertay Harding is about the last damned thing on my mind, dontcha know! I oughta put it on the obit page. With her in charge of the Colony, I can't imagine it will have a long life." Nellie reread the piece quickly, looked up at Rich, and said, "Lord help us with women from New York City!"

Seeing that she was not going to provoke a response one way or the other from her assistant, Nellie moved into editorial mode. She handed it to Rich and looked out her office window while he read. "Good god," he said after reading the last line.

"'Good god' is right. What are we going to do with this thing? Should we try to revise it or just put it out there and let her take her lumps?"

Surprised that there was even an option in Nellie's view, Rich said, "Seems to me that we run it as is. She'll take some lumps from the town folks, to be sure, but you know that, if we change a single word, we'll never hear the end of it."

"You're right about that. The sanctimonious old bat would bitch up a storm. So probably best all round to left her hang herself." Nellie smiled and Rich suspected that such had been her plan all along.

"All righty then," Rich said with a grin playing at the ends of his mouth. "We'll run it as is."

Chapter 37

The result of the hearing and the *Gazette*'s account, letters to the editor, and Art Colony proclamation excited the brains and tongues of Rascal Harbor residents for the next couple of days. As McTavish moved about town, he heard perspectives on both the case and the coverage.

At Lydia's Diner, the mood and the talk seemed to vary from group to group. At least one copy of the *Gazette* was at nearly every table. Where it was being read—in some cases by as many as three readers, each with his or her or copy—the conversations were typically limited to a few interjections and expressions of disbelief. At tables past the reading stage, the conversations were more animated.

"Simon Britton is toast."

"Guess the Park kid really is in the clear now."

"Turcotte don't win 'em all, but he wins the big ones."

"I still wonder if one of them Portlanders wasn't involved somehow."

"Could Mae have her head any further up the chief's ass?"

"How the hell did Lenny get up to Herrington? Last I knew he lost his license and his breath was so bad no one would drive with him."

"What does Nellie do, print letters in dumb-smart-dumb-smart order?"

"You think the chief and Mae might…"

"I know it looks bad for Simon, but I hope it ain't some railroad job cause he's, well, y'know, he's…"

"Jesus, I didn't think Jerry Glenville could put one sentence together, much less four!"

The comments about the case and the letter writers demonstrated some diversity of viewpoint. Such was not the case when it came to assessing the Colony note, which the diner patrons universally attributed to Robertay.

"Christ amighty, that Robertay's got a sense of herself, don't she!"

"What an ass!"

"What a dumb ass!"

"What a friggin' dumb ass!"

"How does Thomas live with that shrew?"

"All them words and they don't mean a thing."

"I can't believe Jona Lewis would have any hand in writing that nonsense. He seems like a reasonable kind of guy."

"This letter hurts the Colony more than it helps."

"Dumb, dumb, dumb."

"Jesus, that Robertay is one stuck-up bitch."

"Why in the hell does she call us 'peaceful residents'?"

McTavish realized that he'd have to slow the eating of his breakfast if he was going to process all of these comments. He wasn't learning anything new about the crime, but he found himself increasingly interested in how and why the town folk thought as they did.

"Christ, Mae Parton's as dumb as you are, Bill!"

This last comment came from Minerva Williams as she passed the men's table on her way to her own. "When Simon 'goes to trial for this robbery!'" Minerva added air quotes to the last part and cackled. "You and Mae related, Bill? Twins born to the same jackass?"

While Bill Candlewith seemed temporarily taken aback, Rob Pownall said, "Down, girl, down!" And Geraldine Smythe called out, "Easy, Minerva, Bill hasn't had his coffee yet this morning. Let him get at least one eye open before you poke the other one out!"

Minerva smiled and took her seat, but not before getting a high five from Karen Tompkins.

"Well, at least I ain't named Minerva!" Bill said, finally coming around.

A moment's silence followed, the nonsense of this remark sent both tables into a tide of laughter and table slapping. Even Slow Johnston joined in, though he wasn't quite sure what the joke was.

"Christ, you got her there, Bill!" Vance Edwards said. "Minerva'll never recover from that one!"

"Minerva, you okay?" June Pickering said through her laughter. "You gonna need counseling now?"

"Don't know about counselin', but I just laughed my ass off so might need a doctor to stitch it back on!" Minerva replied.

At the front of the diner, Julia Nisbett turned to Trudy and asked, "Should we break 'em up?"

"Not yet. Look around." The front-end diners had stopped their reading, their eating, and their chatter, all ears tuned in to the mayhem at the back. "Might sell tickets tomorrow."

McTavish, who was sitting at a table for two, counted himself lucky that he'd neither choked on his donut nor snorted coffee out his nose. Jesus, he thought, maybe Maggie was right. People's lives *are* worth watching.

※

When McTavish stopped for gas at Gary's Garage, he was pulled into the knot of a conversation around the case. Gary, his daughter Louise, and several patrons were chewing hard on Simon Britton, but they did not spare the *Gazette* letter writers or Robertay and the local art crowd. Much of what McTavish heard echoed the sentiments overheard at Lydia's, minus the dust-up between Minerva Williams and Bill Candlewith. As his feelings for the Rascal Harbor residents grew in volume and sensitivity, however, McTavish realized that he was starting to develop deeper insights and to recognize some of the nuance in expression.

For example, while one of Lydia's diners suggested that Mae Parton might be trying to curry favor with Police Chief Miles, Louise offered another perspective: "You know Mae's divorce just came through and, if her former husband is any guide, she's got a thing for paunchy guys with porn star mustaches."

Alan Tuttle added, "Maybe so, but she's also got that son of hers who's one DUI away from losing his license, and then his job. She don't want that kid parking his fat ass on her couch all day, so could be that she's butterin' up old Lawton so's he'll cut the boy some slack."

"Either that or she's angling for a job at the station," said Clint Evans.

McTavish didn't know Mae Parton but, within twenty minutes time, he now had three distinct ideas about the woman based on interpretations of her letter. Is she trying to butter up the chief? he thought, find a new significant other or simply trying to keep her son out of jail and employed? McTavish suspected there might be even more perspectives afloat somewhere across town and was surprised at himself for wondering what they might be. Oh hush, Maggie, he thought as, in his mind's eye, he saw her about to speak.

His musings about Mae and Maggie had taken McTavish out of the conversational stream. When he came back, he realized the topic was now Robertay and the Colony board letter. Again, McTavish heard about the vacuous nature of the missive and the presumptuousness of its author. As he was beginning to realize, however, there was always one more way to look at a situation. He wasn't disappointed.

"Gotta tell ya, that art crowd ain't all it is," Clint said cryptically. Gary and Alan nodded.

Louise looked at the men and said, "What the hell does that mean, Clint?"

"Well, hell, you know, Louise. Don't make me spell it out, you know those arty types."

"I don't know if you can spell or not," Louise said. "And I do know those 'arty types.' Did you forget that Jimmy Park is my brother?"

"No, course not," Clint mumbled.

"Well then, in case you forgot, those arty types go to basketball games, buy gas, and pay taxes! If a couple of them are oddballs and assholes, I can't say that they're any worse than Caleb Rimes. He'd get 'asshole of the year' if there was a vote!" Louise stopped, but before Clint could respond she continued, "And Jesus, Clint, there's another arty type standing right next to you in the form of John McTavish!"

"All right, girl, Clint gets it," Gary said.

"Well, I hope the hell he does." She paused and sighed, "God, sometimes I hate this town." With that, Louise went back into the garage and the Chrysler whose front end she'd been trying to straighten.

The silence that followed Louise's departure broke when Gary noticed Jumper Wilson walking by. "What's your shirt say today, Jumpah?" Gary called out through the open door. Jumper turned, looked in at the gathering, looked down at his shirt, and then opened his coat wide enough so the group could see. On his washed-out, gray shirt, Jumper had written, *The squeaky wheel gets the SHAFT*. Then he did something that no one could ever remember: Jumper slipped off his coat, turned around, and displayed the back of his shirt, which read, *Keep your friends close and…well, just keep your friends close!*

"Truer words," Louise said, as she leaned in from the garage bay. "Truer words…"

McTavish thought that he could continue to gather insights and perspectives if he continued his tour around the places where people gathered in the village. But what he had heard so far was neither enlightening nor salutary. And the fracas between Louise and Clint had depressed him. Should have gone home after the diner, he said to himself as he left Gary's.

GEOFFREY SCOTT

Though the preliminary hearing only settled the matter of whether or not Simon Britton would go to trial, in many residents' mind, it signaled the near end of the case. Folks knew that a trial would ensue and that it would resurrect all the ideas and feelings that had ebbed and flowed over the last month. Still, the verdict could hardly be in doubt. Lee Turcotte was a more than capable prosecutor, the evidence was substantial and compelling, and the police were no longer searching for culprits or clues. The jury may not have decided, but the mass of Rascal Harbor residents had: Simon Britton was guilty of the theft and interest in the incident was already receding. Whether the town would be able to get past some of the other strong feelings surfaced through the events was hard to say.

Chapter 38

The Maine of hard-working fishermen, farmers, and loggers had faded a generation ago. Today, the Maine of tourists and the tourist trade ruled the state economy. In Rascal Harbor, restaurant, bar, and hotel owners, flush with cash from a lively season, made plans to improve and expand their businesses, buy new status symbols, and head south for the winter. Their employees, with a bit more money in their pockets than in previous summers, paid bills, fixed leaky faucets, and bought new second- and third-hand vehicles.

With the preliminary hearing and Simon Britton's indictment fading from immediate view, Rascal Harbor residents found new things to chew on. The high school football team's season wound down into predictable mediocrity, while the basketball team seemed poised for a state championship. Lobster prices had held at a decent level from summer through fall and the upcoming scallop season looked like it might produce a decent yield.

At the retail level, the few stores, bars, and restaurants still open after the traditional post-Columbus Day shutdown were doing an okay business as the fall foliage stayed pretty and plentiful through the last weeks of October. The village didn't bustle as it had during the preceding five months and, for the first time since early June, residents outnumbered tourists. As if freed to take back their town, Harbor folks got out and about and engaged in street-side conversations that lingered a bit longer than they would have during the summer. The locals settled into their post-summer routines and settled in for the coming winter.

McTavish was one of those locals now. He had not spent a late fall and winter in Maine since his college years and he wondered how it would go. Maine winters can sap the life from the most vibrant soul and, with his still battered from Maggie's death and whatever Noah was going through, it began to dawn on McTavish just how unmoored he was from the life he had recently led. His standard definitions of himself—college professor, husband, and father—had all been upended. Only the last role remained and, given Noah's recent visit, it was on new and shaky ground.

The summer bustle, the Homer theft, and a second career in art had all helped get him out of bed in the morning. With the first two motivators waning, he hoped, he really hoped that the third would be enough. Sensing his wife's presence, McTavish said, "Jesus, Mags, it's like I'm a teenager again with a bundle of hopes and fears, new possibilities, and old anxieties. I'll be lucky if I don't end up with a face full of pimples."

McTavish did get up the morning after his visit to the diner and the garage. He was happy to see that his face hadn't broken out. He was less happy about his assessment of the Harbor locals. His reconnaissance of the town post-hearing and indictment had led him to two conclusions—people really did have a myriad of views on any given subject and a good number of those views were petty, foolish, or mean…or all three. McTavish decided he was done with people for a day or two. What was I thinking? he wondered. He got busy before Maggie answered.

Sitting down at his drawing table, McTavish reviewed his recent efforts. The hand drawings that had consumed his attention now felt like they were coming more easily. He wasn't sure that he could put words to it, but he felt a confidence in his understanding of how hands worked and his pencil seemed to follow suit.

What's next? he wondered as he looked through the dozen or so drawings that had escaped the trash can. Faces seemed like the logical step. McTavish had done some decent watercolor versions of faces that he clipped from magazines. He still liked the pieces; he'd even matted and framed a couple. But just as he'd felt about hands, McTavish wondered if the paint had covered up some flaws that would keep emerging until he'd given more serious study to the individual elements.

So maybe I'll allot a week or two to eyes, then noses, and then mouths, he thought. Ears just weren't interesting to him, so he thought he'd let them slide. If I keep that schedule, I ought to feel pretty good about putting a whole face together by spring, he concluded.

As soon as he settled on this plan, however, another thought bubbled up. Concentrating on only one facial feature suddenly seemed enervating and he now realized that he'd avoided sitting down to work on his hand drawings, at times, because he lost interest. He'd managed to get himself back to work, but he now realized that it might be better if he interspersed his focused drawings with some attempts at full-face drawings. Doing so, he reasoned, would break up the drawing day and give him an opportunity to see how his emerging expertise on, say, eyes, fit into the larger composition of a face.

But maybe I ought to take Jimmy's advice and "go all Picasso," he thought, then I can do a good job on the eyes, but just stick a nose anywhere. Shaking off the silliness of that solution, he told himself, it's all got to work together, the pieces *and* the whole.

He hadn't even picked up a pencil, but McTavish felt pretty good about the ideas that were turning around in his head. Good enough, he thought, to stop and have a cup of coffee. Starting toward the kitchen, however, he caught a glimpse of Maggie's face saying, "Really now, John? Taking a break now?"

Maggie's admonition failed to deter him. As he put a filter into the coffee pot, McTavish flashed back to the awkward scene between Louise Park and Clint Evans at the garage. His first thought was, I wonder what Clint would say about the "arty" work I've done this morning.

That idea was followed by a second—I wonder what Clint and Caleb Rimes and some of the other nitwits in town would say about whether there are *gay* eyes, noses, and mouths. Probably.

McTavish mused about such matters while he drank his coffee. He agreed with Louise's assessment that there are "oddballs and assholes" within any definable group. And he had known gay men who shared far more traits and perspectives with guys like Clint and Caleb than they did with people like Simon and Jimmy. Shaking his head at this irony, McTavish mumbled, "Like I said, Maggie, this human being stuff is really beyond me."

Finished with his coffee, McTavish moved over to his drawing table. Before pulling out a fresh piece of paper and taking up the task of drawing eyes, McTavish stacked his hand drawings. As he did so, however, he had a thought. Before he could articulate it, he picked up a light-brown Conte pencil and pulling out one of his hand drawings, he casually drew a large rectangle that encompassed part of, but not all of, the hand. And he smiled. The horizontal-oriented pencil drawing—a right hand bent at the wrist with fingers slightly lifted and pointing to the left—now had a horizontal brown box positioned behind it such that the index finger knuckle, the end of the fingers, the end of the thumb, and most of the wrist were outside of the box.

To McTavish's eye, the drawing now had a kind of grounding that it lacked without the rectangular frame. Though the piece had been more than a simple sketch, it now looked like a real *drawing*. Hmmm, he thought as he pulled out another hand drawing and considered where to place a box that would frame the image. Within fifteen minutes, he had worked all of his pieces into he considered *finished* drawings. In some, the boxes were vertical. In others, he added two boxes. The simplicity of these additions appealed to McTavish's sense of design; the quality that they added to his sketches made him think, maybe he could be an artist. Then he grimaced. "Unless that's a *gay* hand…"

Chapter 39

With renewed interest in his hand drawings, McTavish put away his thoughts about working on faces. He wasn't sure if there was a lot more to do with the drawings; he didn't know if they were worth matting, framing, and trying to sell. But the fact that the simple addition of a penciled-in box had transformed them from sketch to drawing or from drawing to art—he wasn't sure of the language here—fascinated him. How could a few extra lines change everything?

McTavish was mulling through these ideas when Jimmy Park knocked on the kitchen door and came in. "Just thought I'd drop by and see how you were…" Jimmy stopped before finishing the sentence. "What in hell?" he said as he took in the dozen or so drawings. McTavish had displayed them around the kitchen and dining areas so that he could see them individually and as a group.

"I, well, I…" McTavish started to explain, but then stopped as he saw Jimmy slowly and silently take in each piece before moving to the next. The boy toured the gallery of images, then stopped, turned, and stared at McTavish.

"What did you do, John?" Jimmy asked with a sense of amazement.

McTavish, still unsure how to talk about his efforts, simply said, "I…I added a box or two."

"You 'added a box or two'? Jesus, John, you transformed them! You made *art*." Jimmy said effusively. "I mean, they were nice drawings or maybe they were sketches? No, they were drawings…and they were good, but now they're finished pieces, they're pieces of art!" Jimmy stopped, looked back at the pictures. "How did you know to do that? How did you know to add *boxes*?"

McTavish couldn't answer. He suspected there was an answer, some combination of words that would explain what caused him to draw in the shapes, but he didn't know what they were. "It just came to me, James. I was looking at the work I'd done, and suddenly it just seemed right or interesting or necessary to add something, so I penciled in a rectangle on the first one." He pointed to the drawing furthest on the right. "After I saw that I liked it on the first one, I just moved through the rest adding whatever shape or size or number of boxes seemed right."

Here, McTavish hesitated, for he realized that in all of the art talk in which he and Jimmy had engaged, they had never really talked about how they *did* the art they created. They had talked about other artists' use of color and shading, about elements that the artists put in the foreground and background, about the artists' ability to define a focal point. They had talked about their own work and their after-the-fact decisions around drawing versus painting, oil versus watercolor paints, and working with live objects versus working from pictures. They had once spent an hour chewing over the pros and cons of drawing with pencil versus charcoal.

But they hadn't talked about the act itself, the moment when they knew they had done something different to a piece that made all the difference. And now McTavish knew why. He was a man of words, so was Jimmy. But the moment of inspiration, the moment when a new idea struck, it occurred beyond or before or instead of words. It was as if the world were working just fine, and then the next minute it was still working just fine, but a new kind of fine.

McTavish realized that this reverie had pushed him into silence and that Jimmy was now staring at him. He blinked, smiled weakly, and said, "Sorry, drifted off there for a second."

"Where did you go? You were talking about how you made the boxes, and then you were gone. What's that all about?" Jimmy asked in a puzzled and concerned tone. "You okay?"

McTavish smiled weakly again and said, "Yup. Just thinking." Still at a loss to explain his decision, McTavish looked at Jimmy and asked simply, "What do you see?"

"Christ, John, I don't know…they're just different now. It's like you changed the experience of looking at them." He stopped for a moment, then continued. "But one thing I can see is how you created a whole bunch of new negative spaces."

"What do you mean?"

"Don't you remember when Noah was here. We had that big discussion about negative space and how it helps define the positive image that's at the center of the piece," Jimmy said. After McTavish nodded, Jimmy continued. "Well, look at all the new spaces those boxes create that help us see the hand." Jimmy moved to the first drawing and pointed to the four shapes created where the rectangle intersected with the hand. He then pointed to the rest of the white space around the hand and the rectangle and added, "And you've redefined this negative space, too. It was there before, but now it's there differently. Damn, that's pretty cool, John."

McTavish still wasn't sure what to say, so he simply nodded. He thought about Jimmy's notion of something being there and then being there differently.

Chapter 40

As if reading McTavish's mind, Jimmy quietly repeated the phrase, "It was there before, but now it's there differently." Startled that the boy had seemed to reach into his mind, McTavish pulled back. "Huh?"

"Well, that idea, in some ways, is why I came over. It's kind of what I wanted to talk with you about," Jimmy said quietly, hesitating. "But then I saw your drawings, what you did with your drawings, and it kind of blew me away." He paused again. "And then that phrase, those words, just came to me—'It was there before, but now it's there differently'—and that put the point on it for me."

"Put the point on what? I'm not sure I'm following you."

"Sorry, sorry. Can we sit down?"

"Well…certainly. Should I put the coffee on?"

"Oh god, yes, please, but it might help if you could add a dollop from your Bushmills bottle."

Sensing that the boy was about to reveal something big, McTavish nodded and pulled out the Bushmills after he set the coffee pot to brew. Jimmy walked around looking at the drawings again. McTavish leaned against the kitchen counter and watched him. Neither spoke.

After the brewing cycle ended, McTavish poured coffee into two heavy, white mugs, adding a short pour of the Irish to Jimmy's and longer one to his own. Hope I'm not going to need a lot more of this, McTavish thought to himself.

The men sat in the kitchen rockers and quietly sipped their enhanced coffee for a couple of minutes.

"The funny thing is I think you already know what I'm going to tell you. I think you know…" Jimmy said.

As Jimmy's voice trailed off, McTavish turned to him and said simply, "Just tell me."

"Well, John, the truth of it is…well…I'm not a thief…but I am gay."

As McTavish looked at his young friend, Jimmy asked quickly, "Did you suspect?"

"No and yes," McTavish said. "No, I didn't suspect that you stole the painting, or at least I didn't think or want to believe that you did." He paused. "And yes, truth be told, I suspected you might be gay."

"You never said anything, you know, about the gay thing. How come?"

"Well, didn't seem like it was any of my business."

Jimmy considered the older man. "Seems like you're one of the few around here who feels that way. Seems like most everyone else in town's got an opinion about it, whether they say anything or not."

"Must have been hard, knowing that."

"Yeah, maybe it was dumb to hold back on coming out. You're the first person I've told and I gotta tell ya…I know it will sound like a cliché, but it feels like a big weight off me. Just to be able to say it—'I'm gay.' I've practiced saying it so it sounds natural…but…I gotta wonder if it will ever really feel natural," Jimmy said, his eyes misting.

"Hard to know, but I suspect we all suffer a little as we grow into who we are. Some of that growing is easier, some of it's harder, and some of it just takes a long time. It's the growing itself, or how we handle the growing, that probably matters more than the finished product."

"Seems about right. Might be nice though to get someone else to do the growing for you." Jimmy paused before asking, "How do you think it will go with mom and dad and Louise?"

GEOFFREY SCOTT

Holding out his coffee mug, McTavish said with a slight smile, "I think we might need a refill before we go there."

"Yeah, and don't skimp on the Irish this time!" They both laughed and McTavish took their cups to the sideboard.

As McTavish started back with refilled mugs, Jimmy surprised him by standing, stepping forward, and giving him a bear hug. The enhanced coffee sloshed a bit, but McTavish held tightly to the handles. Awkward now, Jimmy stepped back, swiped his eyes, and said, "Thanks, John. Thank you for everything."

Chapter 41

Just as the men resumed their seats and conversation, a hand pounded on the kitchen door and Bradley Little burst in wild eyed and red faced.

"Goddamn it! Goddamn it, Jimmy Park! Goddamn you to hell!"

What coffee McTavish had not spilled before, he spilled now as he jumped up from his rocker. "What in the world....Bradley, what are you talking about? What are you doing here?"

Ignoring McTavish, Bradley rushed toward Jimmy with fist raised, but tears in his eyes. "Goddamn you, Jimmy!"

Stepping between the shocked and unmoving Jimmy and the charging Bradley, McTavish wrapped up the latter, grabbing Bradley's arms and pinning them to his sides. Bradley was taller than McTavish, but slighter. He struggled within McTavish's grasp, but between his wracking sobs and McTavish's adrenaline-pumped arms, the boy's energy quickly subsided.

Through the whole incident, however, Bradley never took his eyes off Jimmy and though most of his words were incoherent, he continued to say Jimmy's name. Realizing that McTavish was not going to relinquish his hold, Bradley slowly slid downward. McTavish held the sobbing boy until they were both on the kitchen floor, McTavish kneeling beside Bradley as he curled up.

Looking up at Jimmy, who had still not moved, McTavish calmly said, "Get a glass of water." McTavish knelt beside Bradley until the boy's sobs softened. Talking quietly, McTavish said, "Stay down, Bradley. It's gonna be okay… Just get your breath and have a sip of water."

As Bradley stopped crying, he pushed himself up to a half-sitting position. He raised his head and wiped his nose with the handkerchief McTavish handed him. Then he took the water glass from Jimmy and swallowed a mouthful, but all without looking at his friend.

"Oh, fuck," Bradley said in a defeated voice. Then shaking his lowered head, he repeated, "Oh, fuck."

Finally finding his voice, Jimmy asked, a bit more stridently than he meant to, "What the fuck is right, Bradley. What the fuck are you doing here? And why did you come charging in here like a goddamn madman?"

Still on the floor with Bradley, McTavish looked up at Jimmy and shook his head to quiet him. "Let's get Bradley up and over on the couch, then we can talk."

Each man grabbed Bradley under an arm and pulled him up. They held on to him as the three walked slowly into McTavish's living room. McTavish sat beside Bradley on the couch, while Jimmy took an easy chair across the room.

Bradley had walked to the couch with his head hanging. He now looked up, first at Jimmy, and then at McTavish. Red-rimmed, his eyes appeared to be misting again, so McTavish patted him on the knee and told him to take another drink of water. The boy complied, then put the glass on a side table.

Looking back down at the floor, Bradley said, "Guess I'm just gonna have to live with it." McTavish and Jimmy waited for Bradley to continue. When he didn't, McTavish nodded slightly to Jimmy.

"Live with what, Bradley," Jimmy said softly. He leaned forward in his chair. "What is it that you have to live with?"

Looking up at Jimmy, Bradley said, "You." And then looking at McTavish, he said, "And you. You two."

Chapter 42

Stunned, McTavish and Jimmy looked at each for a long moment, then they both looked at Bradley. "What?" they said simultaneously.

"Bradley, what are you talking about?" Jimmy asked.

Bradley slowly looked back and forth between the two men, but remained silent for a minute. Then he said, "I guess I have to live with the fact that you two are together. Or maybe aren't together yet, but want to be or will be. I don't know…"

As Bradley's voice trailed off, McTavish and Jimmy looked at one another with questions on both their faces. Finally, McTavish said, "Bradley, do you think that Jimmy and I are more than friends?"

Bradley looked hard at McTavish. "You know you are," he said in a flat voice. "I saw you two hugging, I saw you two." Then turning to Jimmy, he said, "You're always over here. You talk about him all the damn time. 'John says this' and 'John thinks that.'" This latter part, Bradley said in a tired, sing-song manner. Staring at Jimmy, Bradley said, "I mean I had my suspicions when he moved here and you two started hanging around together. All of a sudden you didn't have any more time for me. All you wanted to do was come over here and 'Talk about art,' you said. But I had my suspicions. I'm not dumb you know."

"We know you aren't dumb, Bradley, but we don't know what in hell you're talking about," Jimmy said, with an edge in his voice. McTavish raised his right hand slightly, sending a message to stay calm.

With his voice rising sharply again, Bradley said, "What I'm talking about is that I see what's going on with you two. You want to be together, well, fine with me." With these words, Bradley stood up and started pacing around the living room. "I've always been there for you, Jimmy. When kids used to pick on you, I was the one that got them to stop. I don't think you even knew about that part, did you? You got picked on, you told me about it, and then it stopped. Did you ever think about why it stopped?" Here, Bradley stopped walking and said directly to Jimmy, "Didn't you ever even guess that it was me that was protecting you?"

"I did," Jimmy said softly. "I knew, Bradley."

"I was always there for you," Bradley said again. "And I thought I always would be. I thought we'd be friends, best friends, forever. I thought—"

"But we are best friends," Jimmy said quickly. "Jesus, Bradley, I know what a good friend you've been to me. I know that you've looked out for me. But what is all this nonsense about John? What's he got to do with you and me?"

Bradley stared hard at Jimmy and said, "Fuck you, just fuck you. If you want to be with him… If you just want to be with him, then do it. Just have the guts to tell me to my face. You owe me that."

"For Christ's sake, there's nothing to tell!" Jimmy yelled. "You make it sound like John and I are lovers or some…" Jimmy stopped, hesitated, and then said, "Oh for fuck's sake, is that what you think? That John and I are lovers?"

"Well, ain't you?" Bradley shouted. "You and him? I just saw you. I saw the two of you hugging and hanging on to each other. I saw you!"

"Were you outside watching us?" McTavish asked.

"Of course I was!" Bradley yelled. "Jimmy's been brushing me off, so I wanted to know where he was going and so I saw the whole thing. I saw you two getting all cozy and talking seriously, and then I saw you hug and that was it. That was it! I can't stand it anymore, Jimmy."

"You idiot," Jimmy said loudly. "You goddamn idiot. John and I aren't lovers. Christ, he's straight as an arrow and I'm…I'm…well, goddamn it, Bradley, I'm gay. I just told John and I was asking his advice about how I should talk to my family and, well, everyone else. Then you come charging in here like a goddamn psycho…like a goddamn…" Jimmy stopped and his face went gray. "Jesus, Bradley…Jesus. You came in here like you were jealous. But not just jealous of the time I spend with John, you're jealous because you want me? You want me for yourself?"

Bradley stood still, teary eyes fixed on Jimmy. He nodded.

"Bradley, are you gay? You want me because you're gay, too?" Jimmy slumped down in his chair, his eyes unfixed as he processed this information. He looked up at Bradley and said, "How could I not know this? Am I like the dumbest gay guy in the world?"

Bradley sat down on the couch. "I guess I just thought we'd grow into it. I guess I thought that's what we were doing, you know, just growing into it together. I figured once you got through school and got a job someplace, well, then I could move there, too, and…we could be together. You know, away from all the shit around here."

McTavish, who had sat silently for several minutes, now looked at Bradley, "So when you thought that Jimmy was getting too close to me, you assumed that I was going to take him away from you?"

"Yeah," Bradley said in a defeated voice. "You know, you guys've got art. You're always talking about painting and drawing and shit, and you get so deep, you don't even know anyone else is there. It's like you just *know* each other, you know, closer than friends do. And when I saw you talking like that again today, and then when you hugged, I guess I just flipped."

Bradley leaned back against the couch, the weariness showing in his face and his voice. "Christ, I'm sorry. I fucked this all up. You guys must think I'm an idiot."

"Well, I certainly do!" Jimmy said loudly, but with a trace of humor. "You come in looking like you're going to pound the shit out of me, and then it turns out that you love me! You *are* a fucking idiot." Jimmy stopped, a new thought crossing his brow. "Or shit, maybe I'm the fucking idiot for not seeing any of this coming. Guess I really need some practice with this gay thing. Guess I need to get my gay-dar tuned up."

Chapter 43

McTavish took this moment of calm to announce that it was time for more coffee. He rose from the couch and walked into the kitchen to start a fresh pot and to check the level in his Bushmills bottle. He wasn't sure he'd give any to the boys, but he intended to lay on a good-sized dose for himself.

As he stood in the kitchen, leaning against a counter that allowed him a view of the living room, McTavish watched the boys. Jimmy had moved over to sit next to Bradley on the couch. They did not sit closely together, but their huddled heads and quiet conversation, suggested an intimacy that would have been hard to predict a few minutes earlier. McTavish thought it would be a long road for those two, even if they were willing to try a life together. He wasn't sure he would bet on it. After all, Bradley's temper and jealously, he imagined, could get under Jimmy's skin and his seeming disdain for art could cause an irreparable rift.

Waiting for the last few ounces of coffee to brew, McTavish imagined Maggie's take on the last hour. "I'd have traded places with you in a heartbeat," he said to her. "Christ, Mags, I had no idea what to do."

"And yet, you handled yourself and the situation like a counseling pro," he heard her say. "*You* might not have known that you could do it, but I did."

"Bullshit," he heard himself say, but in his mind's eye, he saw Maggie smile. "Goddammit, Maggie, you think you're so smart." Then he smiled.

McTavish brought unadulterated coffee to Jimmy and Bradley. Returning to the kitchen, he poured himself a healthy, but not immoderate, measure of Irish, and then added coffee. Hopefully I won't need another dose of courage today, he thought.

Walking into the living room and sitting in the chair Jimmy had just vacated, McTavish raised his mug and said, "To friends." The boys toasted as well and sipped their drinks.

"So what's next?" McTavish asked.

"Well, since we've just increased the Rascal Harbor gay population by two," Jimmy said with, "I guess it's time that things become a little more public."

"Bradley, have you come out to anyone else?"

"No, not really. I mean I thought Jimmy knew…maybe I just hoped he knew…but I haven't told anyone."

"So you haven't told your folks either?"

Bradley shook his head. "My dad's been gone a long time, and my mom's about as clueless as Jimmy's."

"Maybe so, but sometimes parents know a whole lot more than they let on," McTavish said.

Jimmy shook his head. "Maybe Bradley's mom does, but Ruby? Jesus, Mom's never had a single thought that didn't come out of her mouth at the same time she was thinking it. I love her dearly, but Jesus… But you can probably guess that it's my dad that I'm most worried about. I expect Louise has guessed it, kind of like, I think you did, John. But my dad? Hard to know what he'll say…or do."

"He better not *do* anything," Bradley said, sitting up straighter and with an edge in his voice.

"Jesus, Bradley, you can't punch my dad into accepting that his son is gay. Besides he could kick your ass three ways from Sunday."

"I'd like to see him try," Bradley said with a growl. "If we're going to be together, then…"

"Wait a minute," Jimmy said with a strain in his voice. "What do you mean, 'If we're going to be together'?"

"What do you mean, 'What do I mean?'" Bradley asked, his color rising. "Jesus, Jimmy…"

"Jesus, Jimmy, *what?*"

"Jesus, Jimmy…I mean I thought you and me…I thought, after all of this." Bradley swept this hand around the kitchen and living room. "After all this, I thought you felt the same way about me that I do for you. Goddamn it, Jimmy, I thought you…I thought you loved…me."

McTavish noticed that both men's faces paled at this comment, though he suspected for different reasons.

Then Bradley's faced reddened again and, with an edge in his voice, he said, "You do love me, don't you, Jimmy Park? Don't tell me I did all of this for nothing."

Jimmy flared. "What do you mean, 'All this,' Bradley? You mean spying on me, pounding on the door, and rushing in here all crazy? Is that what you mean by 'All this' that you're doing for me? I mean, what the hell did you do for me?"

Bradley reddened even more and turned away from Jimmy. He mumbled, "Just, well…" Then turning back to face Jimmy, he said mournfully, "Goddamn, Jimmy, all that I did…it just can't mean nothin'. It just can't." Tears again formed in Bradley's eyes.

Suddenly aware of a twist, McTavish interceded. "Bradley, tell us what you're talking about. What did you do?"

Bradley stood up and walked out of the living room and into the kitchen. He stood with his back to McTavish and Jimmy and slowly started pounding his fist on the countertop. "Goddamn, goddamn, goddamn…" he said with each strike of his fist.

McTavish signaled Jimmy, and the two men walked slowly into the kitchen. Though they couldn't see his face, both of them felt Bradley's anguish. He stopped hitting the countertop, but his whole body started shaking as he turned to face them. The boy seemed to be unraveling. His eyes grew unfocused, the shaking became more violent, and he started crying out in a high-pitched moan. McTavish thought he might be having a seizure, so, for the second time that day, he wrapped him up in a bear-like hug and held him. Immediately, Jimmy did the same thing. For several minutes, they stood in a tableau that would have been incomprehensible to anyone walking by. Bradley shook and mewled; McTavish and Jimmy held him firmly and talked quietly to him in cadences intended to calm.

"It'll be okay, Bradley," McTavish said.

"Relax, Bradley, relax."

Eventually, Bradley began to calm. The mewling stopped first, and then the shaking. But at that point, any reserves Bradley had seemed to leak away and it took all of McTavish's and Jimmy's strength to lead him to a dining room chair. With Bradley seated, they took chairs and waited for him to recharge.

Looking up, wiping his eyes and mouth, Bradley said, "I can't take it anymore. I'm done." McTavish and Jimmy waited. "Jesus, I'm so damn tired," Bradley said, "I just can't keep it up any longer." Jimmy fidgeted, McTavish motioned for him to remain quiet. "It's just…it's just that I thought I was doing it for the right…well, for you, Jimmy," Bradley said plaintively, "I did it all for you…and now it's all gone to shit—"

"For Christ's sake, Bradley, what did you do?"

In a mumble, Bradley said, "I stole the painting."

CHAPTER 44

Though neither man said it, both McTavish and Jimmy thought the same two words: "Holy shit!"

As if they needed the confirmation, Bradley repeated his claim, "I stole the painting."

McTavish would later remember that, with this announcement, Maggie's voice echoed in his ears, "Be careful, John, be careful." Instead of attending to his wife's words, McTavish simply said, "Bradley, do you mean that you stole the Winslow Homer painting?"

With downcast eyes, Bradley nodded. "I did. I took the painting and put it in Jimmy's trunk."

McTavish could see a fire light up behind Jimmy's eyes and his body tense. Fearing that Jimmy would strike his friend, he quietly said, "James, would you go out and get some more firewood? It's going to be cold tonight." The request so surprised Jimmy that he nodded, got up, and went outside.

When he did, McTavish said to Bradley, "Okay, Bradley, I believe you. Shall we go over to the police station or would you like Detective Chambers to come here?"

Bradley seemed to weigh these options without looking at McTavish. Finally, he picked up his head, looked McTavish in the eye, and said, "I owe Jimmy the truth. If it's okay with you, I'd like to tell him here, then I'll go to the station." Bradley held McTavish's gaze with a look that said *please*.

McTavish nodded and thought, Dear lord, there isn't enough Bushmills.

Bradley and McTavish sat quietly until Jimmy came back in with an armload of wood and stacked it in the box next to the wood stove. He came over and sat down at the dining room table beside Bradley. He put his hand on Bradley's, gave it a long squeeze, and nodded to his friend and to McTavish.

And with that, Bradley began. His story rambled at times, lost track of itself at others, and, at still other points, stopped altogether as the man-child wept. There were tears—lots of tears. But there were also accusations and denouncements, aimed at both Jimmy and at McTavish, followed by apologies, most tearfully delivered. McTavish would feel the wrench of this interaction for months.

"I don't know how it come to me, but it did…" Bradley said. "I really didn't intend no harm to come to Jimmy. But I guess I didn't really think it all the way through. Look, I…I was mad at Jimmy. Christ, he was spending all this time with Simon, and then with you, and I…well, I thought I was losing him…" Bradley drifted back into his mind and it was a minute or two before he continued, "I was mad at Jimmy. Here I'd been his best goddamn friend for years, hanging out with him when the other kids wouldn't, and taking on the kids who crossed the line and bullied him. I mean…I guess…over that time, well, I just fell in love with him." Bradley looked long at Jimmy, who nodded, and then continued his story. "I could see how excited he got with Simon and with you, talking art, and hell, I knew I could never do that. But I couldn't give up on him either." Bradley sighed. "So I thought, if there was like some way to show him, to save him, then maybe Jimmy would really see that I cared."

Bradley took a drink of coffee and asked, "John, could I get a little nip added to my cup? This coffee tastes like shit…" The strained nerves that had been building in McTavish and Jimmy eased and they laughed.

"If ever there was a time," McTavish said. He got up, brought back the bottle, and poured a dollop in each man's cup, and another in his own.

Picking up the narrative, Bradley said, "So…like I said, I was mad and confused and frustrated and somehow I thought, if I could just give Jimmy a sign, then maybe he'd see how much I cared." Again, Bradley stopped and took a drink of his coffee. This time, however, he squinted, made a sour face, and said, "Aye, Jesus…John, that was a good pour!"

Bradley took a smaller sip this time and continued. "So that painting and the reception gave me an idea: If I could swipe the painting, make it look like Jimmy did it, and then come in and show how it couldn't be him, you know, kind of rescue him, then…well, then he'd be mine."

Jimmy jumped in. "Okay, but how did you get everything pointing at Simon?"

"Truth be told, a lot of it I just thought up as it was happening, like the ink pad thing. I was going along stampin' those people's hands and when I see Simon in line, it hit me…if I can get his fingerprint on the painting, then I can make him the thief and 'save' Jimmy by lettin' the police know. That's really was as far as I got."

Taking another sip of coffee and growing in confidence, Bradley continued his story. "So I fumbled the ink pad when Simon come along so that he got the ink all over his fingers. I got some on my hand earlier and couldn't get it off so I figured it would make a good mark on the painting. Course it never occurred to me how I was going to get Simon's fingerprint on the painting, but I just kept going with it. You guys know that the painting fell on the floor, but I couldn't see if Simon was over there picking it up or not so I just kept thinking, how am I gonna get Simon's fingerprint on that thing?"

Exhaling, Bradley took a deep breath and plunged forward. "So I was betwixt and between. I'd already let the air out of Jimmy's tire so it would go flat. I figured that would give me time after the show to put the painting in his trunk and I'd looked up the Portland police number so I could leave 'em a tip the next morning."

At this revelation, McTavish and Jimmy looked at one another. They, along with most of the town, had wondered at one point or another, who had tipped the Portland police that the painting was in Jimmy's trunk.

"I figured that I didn't need too much to set up Simon," Bradley said. "I mean, I really didn't want to frame the guy. I just wanted to be able to go to the cops with something that would point in his direction. Then when Jimmy got off he'd see me as the guy who saved him. You know? Maybe it wasn't a great plan, but it mighta worked."

Seeing McTavish and Jimmy shaking their heads, Bradley got angry. "Well, it did! Especially when I got the idea about Simon's key."

"What do you mean?" Jimmy asked.

"Well, when I realized that I wasn't going to get Simon's fingerprint on the painting, I just smudged some ink on the back of it. But I wasn't sure that was going to be enough. I was thinking about it the next day as I was working on Simon's gardens and I got the idea about leaving the back door key so it could be found."

Here, Bradley smiled, apparently thinking himself quite clever: "Maybe the ink thing on the painting would point the police to Simon, I thought, but why not goose it up a little. So when I see Simon's mess of keys, I had the thought to leave his key as a clue."

"How did you know about it?" asked McTavish.

"Cause Simon showed me when he got it. He was pretty proud of getting on the Colony board and his key from Robertay. You know, she made a big deal of handing out the keys to the new board members. And she'd just had it made so it was the shiniest of those on Simon's chains. It wasn't that hard to pick out." Pausing, Bradley sipped more of the very Irish coffee, "So I stole his key, smudged a little ink on it, and tucked it in the grass near the back door of the gallery. I figured if the cops didn't find it, then I'd make another anonymous phone call. That idiot cop Kalin saved me the trouble."

STEALING HOMER

Seeming to smile at his cleverness, Bradley added, "Course, I didn't really know that Simon was in as much money trouble as he is. But once I figured out that it *might* be the case, then I played it up and, it turned out to be true."

"Okay, okay, but how did you know Thomas was going to give me a ride to the garage?" Jimmy asked. "I mean what if Simon had done it? Then he wouldn't have had time to steal the painting."

"Well, to tell you the truth, that was just a lucky thing. I didn't think of it and I couldn't a planned it if I did. You gotta remember that I didn't really want Simon to get hung for this thing. I just wanted enough suspicion so that I could get Jimmy off."

With all the clues accounted for, Bradley's face sagged. Any confidence he'd gained in the telling of his story now left him and he stared at a spot on the table between McTavish and Jimmy. Eventually, Bradley spoke again, "And it mostly worked. Simon got the blame cause all the evidence worked even better than I coulda planned. And I got to seem like the guy who figured a bunch of it out and got Jimmy off. I mean, it was killing me to hold on to that inkpad thing until the cops got stalled. Then I got to 'reveal' it to you guys and you did just what I was hoping—encourage me to go to the cops. I wasn't sure that you bought it all, John, but I could tell that you did." He glanced at Jimmy and then paused a long time before continuing. "You can't imagine how my heart sang then. Seeing your face, you looking at me like I cracked the goddamn case and saved your ass. Me…I was the one who saved you by coming out with that inkpad clue against poor old Simon. You wanted it and I wanted it for you. I thought…well, I thought…maybe this will be the thing that puts you and me together.

"A course it didn't. All it did was give you a clear head so you could start thinking about art again and taking up with John here." Bradley looked quickly at McTavish, sat back in his chair, and thrust his hands deeply into his pockets. "And I could see that that was going to be a problem. Louise told me at the party, but I could see it with my own eyes. You didn't love me. You liked me, but I knew or started to know that you didn't love me like I love you…and probably you never would." He took a deep breath and looked at Jimmy. "So I guess I wigged out a little bit. I followed you around. And I was almost to the point of thinking I might have a chance when you came over here."

Now Bradley looked back and forth between McTavish and Jimmy. "And I saw you. I saw you two…and then I thought…I thought it was never going to happen for us. All my efforts just weren't going to matter. I was losing you…to this fuck!" He pointed at McTavish.

At that point, Bradley looked hard at Jimmy. From his pocket, he drew a switchblade knife, flicked it open, and pointed it directly at Jimmy's left eye. "You won't be no goddamn artist with just one eye," Bradley said, snarling. Without thinking, McTavish punched Bradley in the right ear as hard as he could.

Completely startled and grasping his ear in pain, Bradley yelped and dropped the knife. Immediately McTavish and Jimmy grabbed him, chairs and bodies flying. As the three men hit the floor, McTavish pushed the knife away with his foot while he and Jimmy immobilized the squirming and screaming Bradley.

Chapter 45

The steam left Bradley as soon as McTavish and Jimmy piled on top of him. For the third time that afternoon, he lay on the floor sobbing and curled into himself. No longer afraid for his safety, McTavish let go, motioning for Jimmy to stay with Bradley.

Pushing himself up from the floor, McTavish found the knife, closed it, and put it in his pocket. He grabbed his mobile phone and the business card that Detective Chambers had given him. Taking the phone and the card into his bedroom, McTavish called the detective and told him that he had a "situation" at his cottage that needed immediate attention. He asked Chambers to come by himself, though he suggested that Chambers put the department on alert that the Homer painting thief was ready to surrender.

Walking back into the dining room, McTavish saw Bradley sitting up on the floor with Jimmy beside him, right arm hanging loosely around Bradley's shoulders. Bradley had stopped crying and sat with his head down, drawing imaginary circles on the floor with his finger. Catching Jimmy's eye, McTavish could not read his friend's face. It seemed to register fear, confusion, hurt…and resolve. His first thought was, I'd never be able to capture that expression on paper. His second was, I hope I never have to.

McTavish got a washcloth from the bathroom and wet it with cold water. He started to wash Bradley's face, but Jimmy took it from him. Jimmy slowly lifted Bradley's head and gently cleaned his friend's face. He then folded the washcloth, laid it over Bradley's eyes, and moved Bradley's hand to hold it in place.

Jimmy and McTavish both looked up as they heard a car drive into the dooryard. McTavish walked to the kitchen to open the door for Chambers.

❦

Chambers worried that he was making a mistake going to John McTavish's cottage without backup. *I'll likely catch hell from the chief*, he thought as he entered the driveway. Still, something in McTavish's voice and tone convinced him to come by himself.

Walking into the kitchen, Chambers's face registered surprise as he saw Bradley Little and James Park sitting on the dining room floor. His head hanging down, Little had a cloth covering his eyes. Park had an arm around the other man and a protective look on his face. Chambers had heard McTavish say that the Homer painting thief was at his house. Given this scene, however, he was unsure who he would be arresting.

As he went to help Bradley up from the floor, McTavish answered Chambers's question. "Let's go sit in the living room. Bradley's got something to tell you, detective." McTavish and Jimmy steered Bradley to the couch, where they sat on either side of him. Chambers took an easy chair.

After a minute, Chambers asked, "What have you got to tell me, Bradley?"

Bradley looked up at the detective. His eyes were still red, but dry, and Chambers could see a kind of determination in them. "I stole the painting, detective. And I'm very sorry for it."

For the next twenty minutes, Bradley unfolded the details of the theft and the background behind it. Chambers had advised Bradley of his right to remain silent and to have an attorney present. Bradley had waived these rights. "I just want to tell it," Bradley said quietly.

Chambers listened carefully. He asked a couple of brief clarifying questions, but mostly he let Bradley tell the story. He took no notes. He knew that he'd be hearing Bradley's confession several more times and that there would be plenty of time for notes then.

Bradley's statement included some specifics of the events that occurred at McTavish's cottage. When he described the final struggle, he failed to mention the switchblade. Jimmy looked discretely in McTavish's direction and raised his eyebrows. McTavish's slight shake to the head cued Jimmy that this detail would be their secret.

When he finished, Bradley looked briefly at Jimmy and at McTavish, nodding to both men. Turning to Chambers, he said, "That's it, detective. I'm ready to go now."

Chambers stood, and the others did as well. "I've got to put the cuffs on you," he told Bradley. Jimmy started to protest, but McTavish touched his arm and shook his head. Bradley turned around and put his hands in back of him. "No need, Bradley, you can keep your hands in front of you." With that small concession, Bradley nodded and turned back to face the detective with his hands out. They walked out with Chambers's hand on Bradley's elbow.

Over his shoulder, Chambers said to McTavish, "Give Julian Pratt a call, please, and ask him to meet us at the station."

McTavish recounted the day's events to his sister Giselle on the phone that night. As he did, he had to stop for a minute as recounting the tender way that Jimmy had washed Bradley's face choked him up. "Sorry, Giselle, that one gets me."

"Don't apologize you old dope. Emotions aren't a sin."

"I think I heard Maggie say that once."

"No surprise, brother. I learned the phrase from her." When

McTavish remained silent, Giselle said, "You know, she'd be proud of you John. She'd say you done good."

"Maybe so," McTavish said. "Maybe so."

Chapter 46

News of Bradley's arrest caught the town off guard. Lulled into more pedestrian matters by the wait for a trial, residents were taken aback. As they scrambled to recall the details of the case, opinions became facts and facts became immaterial, but the townsfolk had a grand time. Interestingly enough, rather than build to a consensus view, the chatter ended up supporting a range of perspectives on most every dimension of the case. Even Bradley's confession was suspect in some circles. "He's just coverin' up for that Park kid," one wag announced to both nods and sneers. The only agreement folks seemed to reach was that there was a lot to talk about.

❦

The news of Bradley Little's arrest reached back to McTavish not long after the incident at his cottage unfolded. Half an hour after Detective Chambers drove Bradley to the police station, McTavish's phone rang. "Goddammit, John, it's over!" Gary's voice over McTavish's phone was as loud as it was excited. "I just heard it over the scanner, Bradley Little got picked up for stealin' that paintin'! And he confessed! Goddamnit!"

Because Jimmy was still at his house, McTavish guessed that Gary knew little about how the confession unfolded in general and about his son's involvement in particular. He decided to play dumb. "Oh?" he said. Then he pointed to the phone and mouthed the words, "Your father," to Jimmy. He pushed the speakerphone button and Gary's voice boomed through the cottage.

"Yup, yup, they got him, John. They got Bradley for the whole thing," Gary continued. "I don't know much more than that, but that's got to be good for Jimmy, right? I mean, it's not good for Jimmy cause Bradley is his friend and all…and Jesus, this is just gonna kill Ruby. She loves that boy near as much as she loves Jimmy, but if he confessed and all, then there's really no more way that Jimmy's involved. Right?"

"Hard to see otherwise, Gary," McTavish said.

"Goddamn right. Now I just gotta find Jimmy. He's gonna take this hard, thick as he is with Bradley. Ruby's over at Charlotte's gettin' some new hair and Louise is here with me at the shop. But I gotta find Jimmy. This is gonna be hard on him. Okay, gotta go. Just thought I'd call you first cause, you know, you were there with me in the shop when I first got the call about Jimmy and you, you know, you calmed me down. Okay, really gotta go. See ya."

"Oh boy," Jimmy said, as McTavish clicked off his phone. "Okay if I just hang out here for a little while? Then I'll go face dad and the girls."

McTavish nodded.

Listening to Bradley Little retelling his story at the station, Rendall Kalin was about jumping out of his skin. Jesus, won't the boys down to Henry's get themselves in a right twitch once they hear all this, he thought.

Chief Miles had his own thoughts as he listened in. Why in the fuck did it have to be Bradley Little? he cursed to himself. The boy, especially during his high school basketball days, had sort of reminded the chief of himself at the same age. How could that kid be a fag? he wondered.

After witnessing Bradley Little's confession and agreeing to represent the boy pro bono, Julian Pratt called Paul Reny, Simon Britton's lawyer. "You better get your Portland ass up here, Paul, things are popping."

Gary couldn't wait to tell Ruby. He'd tried to find Jimmy, but to no avail. The boy hadn't shown up at the garage and he wasn't answering his phone. So Gary and Louise drove over to Charlotte's in hopes of catching Ruby. Louise had counseled caution—just because Bradley had confessed did not mean that Jimmy couldn't be accused of being involved. After all, Louise reasoned, everyone knew they were best friends.

"Yeah, but it would have been on the scanner," Gary argued back. "They'd be out looking for Jimmy if they really thought he was involved."

"Fair point, pops, but you know this goddamned town."

Gary turned to look at his daughter. "I do."

Ruby was under the hair dryer when Gary and Louise walked into Charlotte's shop. "Christ, what's that you got around your neck?" Gary asked Charlotte before he could stop himself.

"Mistletoe, you silly old ass." Charlotte cackled and her two missing teeth appeared as an ominous opening in a cave of nicotine-stained teeth. Around her neck appeared to be an entire mistletoe bush. She held it out for Gary to see, then she puckered up and said, "Means you gotta kiss me!"

"Hell, Charlotte, you know I would, but Christmas ain't but for three more weeks. It's bad luck to kiss a girl under…er, around…er, through the mistletoe too early. Santa'll give you the stink eye!"

Ruby had been watching this drama unfold, though she'd only heard about every other word. "What's that about a sinkhole, Gary?"

she asked. "We gonna get all swallowed up like them peoples down in Florida USA?"

Gary held up one hand to ward off Charlotte and another to induce Ruby to stop talking. "I got news," he said loudly. "Louise, get your mother outa that goddamn dryer so she can hear." When Louise complied, she and her father could only stare.

"How you like my new Christmas hair?" Ruby asked with face aglow. "Ain't it something like nobody ever did see before? Charlotte says she's been saving it up for just the right person. And on this very day that right person she chose is me."

Silently Gary and Louise agreed that "Nobody ever did see" a hairdo like that before. Charlotte had left the top, sides, and back of Ruby's head untouched. Instead, she'd concentrated every effort on the front of Ruby's hair. Here, Charlotte had inserted bright red and silver extensions, and then twirled them such that they looked like a row of candy cane icicles. Charlotte then coated each twirl with setting gel. When Ruby shook her head to show off the work, Gary and Louise could hear the pieces clack together like a set of castanets.

"Holy shit," Gary mumbled.

"Holy Christmas shit," Louise mumbled.

At that point, Gary noticed Geneva Baxter sitting in the next chair. Deciding not to feed the gossip beast, he motioned to Louise to get her mother's coat, and they bundled Ruby out the door. They would tell her the news about Bradley when they got home.

Trudy brought all the extra tins of coffee she had at home into the diner the next morning. As Julia helped lug them in from the car, Trudy said, "We're going to need all this and probably more. The gassers will be goin' full tilt today."

She was right. Patrons in both the front and back of the diner lingered over their breakfasts and continually held out their cups as

Trudy and Julia kept the coffee makers humming. Unexpectedly, the two back tables were relatively quiet. Trudy saw both groups huddled in the deepest of conversations, but nary a word leaked into the front of the diner.

Then Minerva Williams and Caleb Rimes came into the diner at the same time. "Here we go," Julia said under her breath.

⚜

Up in Herrington, Simon Britton was ready for a cup of coffee, but he was still in jailhouse clothes and he'd be having jailhouse coffee. His face still wore a jailhouse grimace, but the spark that had been lit with Paul Reny's news was growing. Simon Britton, he thought, do you think you can handle being a free man again?

⚜

Later that morning, the Rascal Harbor Art Colony board met in its second-ever emergency session. The news about Bradley's arrest and confession was still emerging in dribs and drabs, but enough had leaked out that Robertay Harding realized she had a problem.

Robertay had tried, unsuccessfully, to push Simon Britton off the board when she presumed he was guilty. Now that he wasn't, she needed to know how the board felt. Innocent or not, she hoped Simon would just go away so that she would appoint a new member and leave the whole fracas behind. But she knew that Jona Lewis had not appreciated her earlier efforts, and maybe Toni Ludlow was going to be a problem, too. Probably best to test the waters before she made her next move.

Having picked up pastries and coffee, Robertay and Thomas arrived at the gallery twenty minutes before the meeting began. Robertay directed Thomas to lay out the spread while she printed copies of the meeting agenda. She laid out the agenda along with a freshly sharpened pencil in front of each seat. Then she snapped at Thomas, "Good Lord, Thomas, you've put the coffee before the pastries. It goes just the opposite! Otherwise, people will be juggling their coffee while they're trying to pick up their sweets!"

"Robertay, dear, it will only be Jona and Toni joining us. I really don't expect the line will be too long and the confusion too great," Thomas said calmly. Pointing to the other end of the table where the pastries were arranged, he said, "Plus, if they start there, problem solved." Thomas smiled, though not too brightly.

"It's not done that way!" Robertay said, the pitch of her voice rising. "People do not move through a line from right to left, they go left to right! Goddamn it, you are so thick sometimes!"

"I suppose I am, dear," Thomas said meekly and began rearranging the order of the goods.

When Toni Ludlow and Jona Lewis arrived, all was in order and Robertay was seated at the head of the table with a convivial smile in place. "Welcome, welcome, friends," she said a bit too loudly. Sweeping her arm out to the food and drink, she said, "Come and partake before our meeting begins."

Ludlow and Lewis had met earlier in the morning. They had anticipated Robertay's purpose in calling for the emergency session and had talked through their options. They'd both come to their meeting thinking that Robertay had to go as chair and that it would be fitting to have Simon step in. Talking it through, however, they quickly reconsidered. They disliked Robertay, but they could not argue with her ability to run the organization efficiently. They liked Simon, but knew him for a scatterbrain. It would only be fair play to give Robertay the boot and vote Simon into the presidency. But doing so would sink the organization and neither wanted that to happen. So after a bit of reflection, they hit upon a plan: First, Robertay would welcome Simon back onto the board with a small Colony-only reception. And second, Simon would be named the honorary chair of the big spring art show. Stressing the *honorary* part would ensure that the event came off without a hitch and that Simon would have the lead role in the opening ceremony.

They walked into the gallery conference room, smiled at Robertay and Thomas, partook of the pastries and coffee, and settled into their seats. In tandem, they pushed the agendas and pencils aside. Then Toni Ludlow said, "Robertay, this is what we're going to do."

※

Anticipation for the next issue of the *Gazette* almost matched that seen after the preliminary hearing. One might have thought the subject of Bradley Little's arrest would burn out over the several days before the paper came out. Nellie Hildreth considered doing a special edition of the paper the day after the confession leaked. She didn't think she could round up enough advertising to support the cost, however, so she opted for a big headline on the front page of the regularly scheduled edition.

Nellie gave Sarah McAdams her head in terms of writing the lead story. The journalist came through with a reporting gem that clearly outlined the complex story and presented Bradley Little in fair fashion. Because Detective Chambers had left it out of the official report, McAdams gave few details about the drama that occurred at McTavish's cottage. She concluded her story with sufficient attention to the range of public viewpoints to suggest that Bradley's confession was far from a singular resolution to the issue.

The letters to the editor confirmed the diversity of perspective evident in Sarah's article such that everyone in town could both nod and scoff at the intelligence and stupidity of their neighbors and friends. Oh, and predictably, the Red Sox got a measure of attention.

Maybe the piece that got the most notice, however, was Nellie's *not quite* obituary for Simon Britton:

Requiem for an Almost Goner

Simon Britton, somewhere north of 50, is again among the living. Given up on by a sizable portion of the community and some of his so-called friends, Simon got back his freedom, if not all of his life. We have all known the sting of accusation. When it's true, we deserve the sting; when it's false, nothing can quite dull the barb. Simon deserves a big apology starting with the Rascal Harbor Police Chief. Of course he won't get it, but he should.

Sober reflection would suggest we all take the lesson that rushing to judgment is almost always a piss-poor idea. Of course we won't and the next time it happens, and there will be a next time, we'll likely go through the same nonsense all over again. Just maybe, though, a few folks won't jump so hard and fast. And, if that is the case, in about a million years, we human beings might actually act consistently in humane ways.

Oh, and anyone who knows Simon, knows he loves flowers, so feel free to send him a bunch with a nice written card. It's the least we can do.

Breaking with prior practice, Jumper Wilson wore his latest T-shirt for a solid week, over his coat rather than under it. On the front of Jumper's shirt, he had scrawled, *Never put off today what you can be accused of doing the day after.* The back read, *A friend in need is a friend shit out of luck.*

Chapter 47

Giselle tipped off the rest of the McTavish siblings about the resolution of the case. Her email left out most of the drama that occurred at the cottage on the assumption that her brother ought to decide what and how much he would reveal.

McTavish was judicious with those details when Mark and Ruth called. They were at Mark's house using the speakerphone. McTavish assumed that their respective spouses and children were somewhere in the background, but his brother and sister gave them no air time. Mark and Ruth had questions and they intended to get them answered.

"Jesus, brother, some kind of crazy scene up there, eh?" Mark started.

"So it would seem," McTavish responded evenly.

Mark pushed on. "So did this all really happen right there at your cottage, the whole scene blew up right there?"

"My goodness, John. It must have been terrifying to have this criminal right there in your living room. Was it your living room? Or kitchen...?" Ruth asked.

Realizing that he was going to have to feed the beast at some point, McTavish said, "It was in the kitchen, mostly. The boy, Bradley, well, he just kind of came apart, so his friend Jimmy, James Park, and I just stayed with him until the police arrived."

"His *friend?*" Mark scoffed. "The Portland paper said something about it being a kind of crime of passion. They said that the Bradley kid did the whole thing as a way to show the Park kid that he...well, he—"

"*Loved* him!" Ruth said. "There weren't many details, but that's what it sounded like. Is that what it was, John? Honestly, some people…"

"I'm not sure we'll ever really know," McTavish said, hoping to forestall the exploration of Bradley's and Jimmy's sexuality. "All we really know for sure is that Bradley confessed to the theft of the painting and now the fellow who was in jail is free and clear, as is Jimmy Park."

Mark said, "That Simon fella, he's one of those—"

"Homosexuals!" Ruth said, interrupting again.

Not for the first time, McTavish thought that his brother and sister really were two sides of the same coin. "Yes, Simon is a gay man, but he's innocent of this crime and that's the important thing," McTavish said.

Mark scoffed again. "Ah, Christ, Ruth, we aren't going to get anything out this brother of ours, we'll have to wait until we see him next time. If we can get a little bit of the Bushmills in him, maybe that will loosen up a little more of the story."

After McTavish hung up with Mark and Ruth, he promised himself that he'd stay some distance from the Irish the next time he saw them. He turned to the kitchen sink where his lunchtime dishes awaited his attention. When his phone rang again, he was tempted to let it go to voicemail as he imagined it was Mark and Ruth trying out a new angle. Leaning over to confirm his suspicion, McTavish was surprised to see his son's name on the display.

"Noah, are you okay?" McTavish asked with a hint of worry in his voice. Though they had not spoken since the scene at the Portland airport, McTavish had thought about reaching out several times. *If I could just figure out the first words to say,* he told himself. Maggie, of course, had been no help at all. Each time he failed to make the call, McTavish's mind had gone instinctively to Maggie. They had talked several times. Each time McTavish surprised himself at how much he was willing to reveal about his feelings towards his son, both good and bad. Maggie had listened, asked questions, and softened some of McTavish's harshest self-criticism. She would not, however, tell him how to approach Noah.

"Sorry, John McTavish, but you're just going to have to figure that one out on your own," she'd said each of the several times he had asked for her guidance.

"Goddamn it, Mags," he'd said at one point. "You know that I want to get this right with Noah and you know that I'm more than likely to muck it up without you."

"You might, you just might. You haven't got a great track record so far, but the only way that you and Noah are going to come to terms is if you put yourself out there to Noah. Your real self, John. Look, this isn't some kind of test. I'm not answering because I'm waiting for you to guess the way I'd respond. I expect that's what you've been doing, and I'd bet dollars to donuts, especially Lydia's molasses donuts, that that's why you're stumped. I can't tell you what to say to your son because I could only tell you what *I* would say to him. You've got to figure out what *you* want to say."

The human mind amazed McTavish. This entire exchange with Maggie had buzzed through his head in the fraction of time between seeing Noah's call come in and his question to Noah about being okay.

"I'm fine, Dad," Noah said. "I was just wondering about you." Noah explained that he'd been tracking the Homer theft case online and through text messages with Louise Park. "I knew you weren't going to call, so I decided to do so."

"Thanks, it's been a little nutty around here of late."

"Sounds like it. Louise said that it was a wild scene there at the cottage. She said Jimmy's talked about it non-stop. You're like his hero."

"Hero?" McTavish asked.

"Yeah, according to Jimmy, you were one cool customer, especially when you punched that Bradley kid and got the knife away from him. Hey, that reminds me, how come there was no mention of the knife in any of the reports?"

"Guess it didn't seem like Bradley needed any more trouble."

"Jesus, Dad, you saved Jimmy's life, or at least his eye, and all you're thinking about is not causing this nutcase any more trouble?" Noah said, disbelief in his voice.

"It all happened pretty fast. I'm not sure there was a lot of thinking involved." Pausing, McTavish turned the conversation. "Did Louise say how Jimmy is doing? I haven't heard much from him since it all happened."

"I guess the family kind of hunkered down once Jimmy explained just why Bradley did what he did. Louise said he did a pretty good job coming out to them. Of course it helped that they were lucky to still have him alive and in one piece. As you might guess, Gary is having the hardest time. But Louise said that, when Jimmy told them he was gay, it was almost like Gary could finally breathe…you know, like he'd been holding his breath in for years and now could finally let it out. Louise said it was pretty weird and definitely awkward for a while, but she thinks it's all going to be okay."

"How did Ruby take it?"

"Louise said Ruby actually took it all pretty hard, though she wasn't sure whether Jimmy almost dying, Jimmy being gay, or Bradley being the thief was the most upsetting. Guess she kept saying, 'I knew that Bradley would do anything for Jimmy, but I didn't ever never even think something crazy dumb like this.' Louise says she still isn't quite sure that Ruby gets the whole gay thing, but she'll keep trying to explain it."

"Sounds like you and Louise have been doing a little more than exchanging texts," McTavish said with a hint of a smile in his voice.

"Don't try to deflect the conversation…but yeah, we've been talking. She's cool."

STEALING HOMER

"She is, Son."

McTavish and Noah concluded their conversation with talk about Noah's upcoming finals. Noah startled McTavish by saying that he planned to come to Rascal Harbor for the semester break. McTavish hid his surprise and they talked through Noah's flight times and made a plan for McTavish to pick him up at the airport. After they hung up, McTavish said, "Well, what do you think about that, Maggie McTavish?" Maggie only smiled.

Chapter 48

A week later, McTavish drove to the Portland airport. He and Noah had not talked since their last call, but they'd exchanged texts confirming Noah's flights and arrival time.

After the second time he had had to wipe the sweat from his palms, McTavish realized that he must be nervous. "What could I possibly be anxious about?" he asked himself with a tight smile. "Everything went so swimmingly the last time Noah was here…and this time he'll be home for three weeks…"

McTavish's mind conjured up Maggie's image, but she said nothing.

Noah greeted his father with a modest smile and a good, if not great, hug. McTavish reciprocated and they walked to the car discussing the weather, the flight, and a funny scene Noah witnessed between a grandfather and his young granddaughter on the plane.

"She asked him if there were planes around when he was a kid," Noah said. "He told her there were, but they were powered by winding up big rubber bands. The little girl said, 'Cool beans, Grandpa!'"

In the car, Noah asked for an update on the theft of the Homer painting. He'd heard that the value of the painting was unclear, but the bizarre story behind the crime was likely to ratchet up the auction price. McTavish said he'd heard the same thing but, he'd also heard that Robertay Harding had asked the owners to donate it to the Art Colony permanent collection.

"Jesus, is she nuts?" Noah asked.

McTavish responded simply, "Ayuh."

Noah laughed. "Ayuh? You're getting your Maine accent back, I see."

"Indeed, my boy! Indeed, I am!" McTavish said, now in an exaggerated English accent.

A short silence ensued. Noah broke it by asking how Simon Britton was doing after his release from jail.

"Not great. I've seen him a couple times in passing and he just looks adrift. He's lost weight, his color runs to gray, and he has a hard time looking people in the eye."

"Jesus, jail really did a number on him," Noah said.

"So it would seem. I know that the Art Colony folks are trying to get him back on track. He's going to be the honorary chair of the spring show. But I think it's going to take more than that. Turns out he really was having money issues and so he's got that to deal with, too."

"Don't suppose he could sue anyone to pay for his false arrest."

"No, not really. I'm sure he and his attorney talked about it but, from everything I can see, the police did what they could with what they had. I don't trust the chief a mite, but I think the lead detective played fair."

"Small consolation," Noah said.

McTavish just nodded.

A couple of minutes later, Noah asked, "How's the art going?" In a slightly teasing voice, he asked, "Still on the hands?"

"As a matter of fact, I am, wise guy," McTavish said with a smile. He explained the inspiration about adding the framing boxes to his initial drawings and how they seemed to transform the work.

"No kidding. I'm not quite sure I understand what they look like."

"I'm probably not explaining it very well. Jimmy thinks the difference is that the boxes increase the number and quality of the negative spaces around the hand images…and that that increases the interest."

Geoffrey Scott

"Hmmm, negative space again, huh? Funny how that idea keeps popping up."

"Yeah…I guess it does." Halfway to the cottage, and after another short silence, McTavish looked over at Noah and said, "It'll be nice to have you home."

"Home? Not sure I've ever heard you use that word before to refer to the cottage. You really are settling in."

"I suppose I am," McTavish said. "Maybe I never really left Maine all those years ago."

"How do you think your life would have turned out if you'd stayed?"

"Hard to say. Can't say I've given it much thought until just now, but if I hadn't left, I wouldn't have met your mother and I wouldn't trade that for anything."

"Really?" Noah asked with a tinge of skepticism.

McTavish paused before answering. A wave of emotion ebbed through him as he wondered what Noah meant by the question. He bit back a sharp response and said simply, "Yes, really. But why do you ask it like that?"

Retreating a bit, Noah said, "Oh, it's not that I doubt that you loved Mom. It's just that, well, a whole lot of other stuff came with marrying her. The life you two made there…me." Noah looked straight at his father with this last word, but he said it plaintively.

"And I wouldn't trade anything for *all* of that either, Noah." McTavish looked at his son. "All of it."

"Well, I know that *some* of it—namely me—has come with a shitload of baggage that I know, for a fact, gets on your every last nerve. Gets on my every last nerve, too, sometimes."

"I suppose we just have to try to figure it out. Your mom was always saying something like that."

"I think what she said was, 'All we can do is try to grow into the people we're supposed to be.'"

"Ayuh, that was it," McTavish said with a full smile. Noah smiled, too.

After a pause, Noah said, "So…maybe there's some stuff we can work through to get to be the people you and I are supposed to be."

"Ayuh."

The End

Geoffrey Scott

is the pseudonym of **S. G. Grant,** a professor of history education at Binghamton University. Grant has authored or edited nine education-related books and numerous articles and book chapters. This is his first work of fiction.

Made in the USA
Columbia, SC
11 May 2018